Body of Water

The Orcadian Novels

Book One

Stuart Wakefield

DEDICATION

This book is dedicated to my sister, Lisa, for always believing in me.

ACKNOWLEDGMENTS

An ocean of thanks to:

My wonderful friends, for all their love and support.

Kate Tenbeth, who turned her light up brighter when mine started to flicker.

My long-distance pal, Laura Lee Price, for spotting the typos I missed.

Mara Ismine, for reading it of her own accord and giving me some great advice.

My peers: the gang at Writebulb, Penelope Fletcher, Josephine Myles, Charlie Cochrane, Clare London, Kay Berrisford, Alex Beecroft, Erastes, Sam Leonhard, and everyone in the Goodreads M/M Romance group.

CHAPTER ONE
VORE TULLYE

She sat on the empty beach, burrowed her feet into the warm sand, and looked out across the sea. The setting sun seemed to bubble in the water, sending out ripples towards the shore.

From the moment she had discovered her pregnancy, her attraction to the ocean had been so powerful that it overwhelmed her. A water birth was all she could think about apart from getting away from her husband, Mackay, the knight in shining armour who had proved to be a metal-plated misogynist.

Mackay was aggressive and controlling, but she had been determined, as was the custom in Orkney, to conceal her birth from the evil spirits.

If only she had succeeded; Mackay wasn't the father.

Reaching up to her chest, she held the star sapphire pendant in one hand. In the twilight, the way the stone reflected sunlight wasn't visible but she didn't care; holding the stone made her feel closer to the only person she had ever trusted in her mortal years, and she drew strength from it in her darkest days.

She wondered what its original owner would have made of the leather thong threaded through the pendant instead of the beautiful metal chain it had once hung from. Shuddering, she recalled the moment when the chain broke. Mackay had discovered the pregnancy and, knowing he could never have been the father, grabbed her by the throat and punched her until she fell unconscious. The chain broke when she sank to the ground.

Today had been unusually warm and her dress felt as heavy as her mood. The cool evening breeze dried the sweat on her brow but she still felt uncomfortable.

Hoping that the beach would remain empty for the time being, she wriggled out of the garment. Free from its weight, she felt as light as the gentle wind that now lifted and curled her blonde hair around her neck and shoulders.

Her tummy rumbled. She had forgotten to eat again. This had become a common occurrence in the past few days as she plotted her escape. A new life with her baby, far away from the island, seemed possible. The only thing that kept her here; pinned her down to this place was the ocean's pull. Its pull was strong.

Very strong.

That rumble again, slightly painful this time. She drew her knees up to her bosom to ease the discomfort and felt a sudden wetness between her thighs.

Her anxious heart pumped hard and her breathing quickened. She reached out for her dress but another cramp doubled her in two. Incredible pain blurred her mind. What should she do? Call out for help? She doubted anyone on the cliff-top would spot her down on the beach, let alone hear her cries.

She had a ready-made birthing pool right here but she hadn't planned on being alone. Would He come for her if she entered the water? She needed a midwife. She needed protection.

The next cramp unleashed her voice but the only response was her own cry echoed from the cliff behind. She would have to take care of this herself.

Raising herself up onto her elbows, she shuffled her swollen body, feet first, towards the water. The exertion made her sweat anew but she only had a few yards to go before her domed stomach was partially submerged.

At once, the water relaxed her, allowing her to turn her focus inwards. She concentrated on pushing, remembering what she had learnt from the one local woman who knew of her condition.

Sensing that something had changed she opened her eyes again. It was dark, but so soon?

The water was completely still. The ocean, once bursting with movement and sound, now stretched out before her like ink on a mirror, reflecting the newborn stars above. Even as she laboured in the water, the ripples only spread a couple of inches before dying out.

She had seen this once before.

He was coming.

Two lights winked into existence just beneath the water's surface, the same colour as her star sapphire in daylight.

He was here, watching her. Waiting.

Feeling sudden warmth on her chest, she looked down to see her pendant shine, illuminated from within. Its rays emanated gently from the stone's core.

She had been right about its power; the effect soothed her. Smiling, she laid back and let the warmth envelop her body. She imagined the midwife with her now, holding her hand, giving her gentle encouragement and calm instruction.

The water came alive around her and quietly carried her body further out. Just a few feet from the sand she felt it working around her, applying mild pressure to her abdomen. A few feet more and her uterus opened. She closed her eyes again, feeling the new efficiency in her body. The living water did not scare her; the ancient magic was at work.

Time passed and her miracle was complete. It had taken longer than she realised; a thin slice of sun peeked over the horizon, the first thing to bear witness to the birth of her baby boy.

She floated on the surface and the boy lay across her chest. Warm water caressed them both, cleansing their skin, soothing their cries and separating them. The warmth felt like love itself and it teased out the human emotion she had fought so hard to cultivate. She cried for the pain she suffered at the hands of a man who never loved her, for the inexplicable guilt at wanting to leave this world, and for what she knew was about to happen.

He broke the surface of the water a hundred yards from where she floated. In one movement, she turned to her side, her legs sinking beneath so she was upright, and her child was cradled against her breast.

She knew what He wanted.

The boy arched in her arms, eager to be free. She hesitated for a moment, fearing not only for his safety, but also for her loss.

She thought about the life the child would have with Mackay as a father and released him. Her son darted through the water towards Him making an unfamiliar sound with what seemed like greater and greater excitement.

Finally, the boy reached Him. Seeming satisfied that the boy was in a healthy condition, He swam towards her.

As soon as He had appeared, she'd recognised Him as the man she had found unconscious on the beach. His skin had been as deathly pale as the sands on which His body rested. Shocked to see a stranger washed up on the shore, she had immediately wrapped Him in her coat before trying to revive Him. His hair, jet black, clung to His neck and, having tucked it behind one ear; she had been stunned to find three small slits in His neck.

Propping Him up against her, she spoke urgent words of encouragement into His ear. She breathed in His scent, pure as the ocean she loved.

He had regained consciousness after some time, distressed to find Himself on land. He breathed instinctively through the slits in His neck but this made Him dizzy. She persuaded Him to breathe through His mouth to keep from passing out again. In broken English, He explained to her that He had been caught stealing and cast out of His underwater community.

She had promised to return each day until He was strong enough to go back to the ocean.

The day He left, she had swum out into water with Him. They made love then; a love that she had borne inside her since.

He was close now, treading water before her. His eyes blazed blue even in the daylight, His sneer communicating His disgust even before He spoke. "You have spent so long living as one of them that you have forgotten who you are."

"You are mistaken. My mind is like water and, although my memories are diluted, they are never truly dissolved. I remember myself now, as I remember you. I shall return in time but for now you may take this child and care for him."

He changed then, shifting from His human form back to the creature that she had fought through the ages. "I will wreak havoc in your absence!" He cradled the child in one arm and struck the water with His free hand. Immediately the ocean began to churn around them. Clouds rolled in to fill the sky and lightning struck the shore.

The deafening roar of thunder did nothing to alarm her and, even as the water rose up around them, creating a huge circular wave, she did not flinch. With a sweep of her hand the water calmed. "You always did, my love, and you always will."

Too angry to speak, He took the boy and left.

Alone again, she began her swim back to the shore.

The discovery of her clothes on the beach was enough for the authorities to conclude a verdict of accidental death.

But one woman knew better.

CHAPTER TWO
BEGINNINGS

Every night I have the same dream.

I am five years old and full of fear and anger. The sun burns down on me as I stand on the crispy grass in front of the children's home. The man who lives across the street is running towards me, shouting. Spittle foams at the corners of his mouth, like an animal. This fascinates me. My mouth is dry. My lips feel tight and sore. I wish my mouth was wet like his.

No, he is not running towards me. He is running towards the dog lying at my feet. His big, scary dog that always barks at me. It is not barking now. It is still. I know I stopped the dog barking and I smile at my triumph.

"He's dead!" The man begins to cry and struggles to lift the dog into his arms. I want to touch his face. He looks at me and gasps. The man looks scared and I enjoy his fear.

The dog's head slips from the man's arms and water pours out of its mouth onto the yellow lawn.

I hear someone come out of the house and soon their hands are on my shoulders, guiding me back inside.

My real mother is the person who takes me back inside the house at the end of my recurring dream.

I am as sure of that now, just as I was as a child, even though the staff at the children's home couldn't answer my questions. All they would say was that she gave me up for adoption and promptly disappeared.

Ruth, the woman I would eventually call Mum, came into my life years later when she volunteered to foster me.

Even from our very first meeting Ruth was always different. When she smiled, she did so naturally, whereas so many women before her had looked uncomfortable. They'd been warned in advance. Michael, as I was known then, was difficult and, no doubt, different.

"I'm Ruth." She sat down, not opposite me, but to the side. Her unusual accent caught my attention at once. It was a bit like mine.

"Where are you from?"

"Orkney."

I shrugged. I'd never heard of it. Then I noticed the man with her, tall and thin, bursting with nervous energy. "And I'm Alex." He thrust his hand towards me. I ignored it. He was a Southerner.

"Do you already have children?" I said to her.

"No."

"Are you sterile?"

"No." She looked so comfortable, so calm.

"So it's his equipment that's on the blink?"

Alex gagged.

"I'm just too lazy to have a baby." She widened her eyes in self-deprecation. "All that dreadful backache and eating coal."

"Have you fostered before?"

"Yes, eleven times. Ten children and one dog."

"The dog doesn't count."

"Well, another mother gave birth to her and then she was my baby."

"But you bought her."

"Actually, we rescued her."

"I don't need rescuing."

She considered this for a long time and a silence fell upon the room. "Don't you?"

Oh, she was good. I'd have to find something else to put her off. "I'm not nice."

"Who wants nice? Nice is boring."

7

"And you can't treat me like a fucking dog." That had to do the trick. Who wanted a nine year old who swore like a sailor? Ruth appeared anything but flustered.

Alex leaned over and whispered to me conspiratorially. "You might change your mind after you hear how she treated the fucking dog. Trust me; you'll get more attention than I do."

I liked them. Her more than him but he was funny. I could see why they were together. They cracked jokes and didn't take themselves too seriously. With her accent I would fit in if people didn't know us. They still needed testing.

Three months into my placement with them and they still hadn't cracked. I knew I should ease up but my compulsion to misbehave, to find out how much they were prepared to live with, was too strong.

I spat in my dinner if I didn't like it, then I spat in theirs. I lashed out at them when they reprimanded me. Most nights I sneaked out of my room to hang out with the rough kids on Primrose Hill.

But Ruth seemed impervious to my wrongdoing. She regularly picked me up from the local police station, oozing charm and issuing apologies to all concerned. A quiet word with the sergeant and everyone would be smiling. We were usually on our way within a few minutes.

"What do you say to them?" I said the last time, my feet up on the dashboard of the car.

"I tell them what you're really doing."

"What's that?"

"You know what; now put your feet down."

How could she know me so well? We drove in silence but she caught me looking at her a few times. She smiled at me and patted me on the leg. We didn't need to speak.

When we arrived home, we were greeted by an agitated Alex. Ruth kissed him and told him everything was fine, that I was exhausted and I was going to bed straight away.

Any potential unpleasantness between Alex and me waited until the morning but in the meantime Ruth smoothed things over.

Finally convinced of their love for me, I settled. I became popular enough at school with both sexes and that granted me a relatively easy time there. I worked hard to make up for a disjointed education and Alex employed a personal tutor to help bridge the gap.

The more praise Ruth gave me the harder I tried. Alex, although present and equally encouraging, seemed on the periphery of everything, spending most of his time at work.

Ruth seemed happy enough with the situation but I could see that she was happiest when we were all together. She called us 'my boys' and I, by the time I started secondary school, became Leven, a nickname representing the eleventh child they'd fostered.

Alex was hardly an absent father but he wasn't as close to me as Ruth. During his rare days off we would do all the things he thought a father and son should do. He taught me some basic woodwork, how to hang wallpaper, and he talked about sport.

Try as he might, by my mid to late teens I still wasn't into sport but I became mesmerised if I happened to flick through the television channels and see the men's diving. My heroes teetered on the edge of the board, their muscles flexed, launching into beautiful, impossible shapes before plunging into the water.

At first I felt nothing but admiration for them but, the older I became, the more I felt something else too. My face would flush when certain divers took to the board and I'd feel the heat creep down my body.

Later in bed I'd think of those particular divers and the heat would return while I wondered what they'd feel like to touch.

I pleaded with Alex for diving lessons but he was swift to remind me that I couldn't swim and had little prospects of ever doing so.

"So get me some swimming lessons!"

"How many times must we go over this?" Alex said, his head in his hands. "Mum will never let you near the water."

"It's not fair. Why do I have to pay the price for her parents being drowned in sodding-"

"Lev-"

"-frigging-"

"Leven-"

"-fucking-"

"Leven!"

"ORKNEY?"

"Sorry mate, it's just not happening. Why not try skateboarding?"

I stomped off up the stairs.

"And don't stomp off up the stairs. You know there's a dodgy bit of plumbing – oh Christ!"

I knew just the spot to hit to crack the pipe and keep Alex occupied with repairs for the rest of the day.

A few weeks after my sixteenth birthday, one of the girls at school had a party to mark the end of the school year. Her parents had given over the entire basement of their Georgian house to her and it had been converted into a self-contained flat.

Late in the evening, the drinking games started and she arranged us all into a circle, boy-girl, boy-girl.

"It's the ice cube game," she slurred as she fumbled with the trays to loosen the contents. "You put an ice cube in your mouth, right, and pass it around the circle."

Several cheers went up from the rugby team and several more groans from the girls sandwiched between them. A boy with braces looked mortified, made his excuses and went home.

Having never kissed a girl, nor wanting to, I felt mildly uncomfortable as the ice cubes came and went but it was clear that everyone else was having a great time.

Towards the end of the game, there were multiple cubes in play.

When the girl between me and the captain of the rugby team clamped her hand over her mouth, retched, and rushed to the toilet, a huge roar went up.

Expecting another girl to take her place, I swallowed hard when I saw an ice cube heading towards me. The rugby captain, someone called him Shaun, took it and leaned towards me. The roar was deafening when our mouths met.

But there was no ice.

He made a spectacle of passing it over, and I, in my innocence, searched for it with my tongue before I realised what I was doing. As I withdrew my tongue from his mouth so his ventured into mine.

It wasn't how I'd imagined my first kiss. It should, I thought, follow the private declaration of eternal love from my Olympic diving, gold-medal-winning lover, not a drunken rugby joker surrounded by a baying mob of his team-mates. As soon as the length of the kiss threatened to become obvious to even the most pissed observer, he pushed me away, laughing. His good-natured jokes diverted any embarrassment on my part.

He didn't avoid me afterwards. If anything, he seemed friendlier than ever, throwing his arm casually around my shoulder when I found myself sitting next to him on a wall while he had a heated, if slurred, debate with his friends about the distinction between tackling and rucking.

I didn't see him again that summer and, as the next school year began, I found out that he'd transferred to a boarding school.

Months later, as spring breathed life back into nature, I saw a red-haired girl leave the house across the road. It wasn't her hair that caught my attention but the fact that she'd left the house at all. For over a year the house had been undergoing considerable renovation. I'd become so used to the noise of activity over there that I'd missed her family finally moving in.

She dressed eccentrically. The cuffs and collar of an unremarkable jumper were stuffed with fluorescent netting. A short tartan skirt skimmed her hips and mismatched tights led the eye down to her platform trainers. She beamed up at me when she saw me at the window and I quickly stepped back, embarrassed that she'd seen me watching her.

A moment later I heard a knock at the door.

"Hello," a girl's voice said, as Ruth answered.

"Hello. Bethany, isn't it?"

"Yes. I was wondering if your little boy might like to come out and play? I saw him watching me."

The silence underlined Ruth's utter astonishment. To my horror she complied. "Just a moment, I'll ask him."

I groaned. Ruth was kind to a fault, always volunteering me to do some good deed that I had no interest in. Even as I had the thought I felt guilty. Why couldn't I be more like her? I might complain about doing the things that she volunteered me for but once I was doing them I always felt better about myself, and happy to have pleased her. I fought with these feelings on a daily basis.

"Darling," Ruth said lightly as she peeked around my bedroom door, her face contorted with trying not to laugh. "Bethany-"

"I prefer Beth, actually," yelled the girl.

"Sorry. Beth is asking if you'd like to come out and play." Ruth was enjoying this too much.

Incredulous, I groaned again. "Why? She's like, what? Nine?"

"I'm fourteen," the voice bellowed from downstairs.

"She has an older brother. He's about your age. Maybe if you went over there you might make a new friend?"

"I don't want to make a friend." That much was true. I liked this little world we had here.

"All right, darling. I'll tell her."

Ruth was barely half-way downstairs when my inner struggle began. I had no friends outside of school; that much was true. What harm would it do if I just went over there and had a look around? I'd explored every inch of this place and although I loved it here, a part of me was curious enough to go and find out.

Just as Ruth got to the door, I pushed past her and ran down the steps onto the pavement.

"Come on, then," I said. "Let's go."

"Darling," Ruth called after me. "Have you got your. . .?" She tapped her chest.

I tapped my chest to confirm that I was wearing the pendant she had given me, insisting that I wore it at all times.

Ruth and Alex's house was beautiful inside, classic in design, but warm and inviting. Beth's house was something else entirely.

Palatial didn't quite cover it. Marble floors stretched ahead of us and the most gigantic glass chandelier I'd ever seen hung over us, suspended from a chain that looked too feeble to carry its massive weight.

"Do you like it? Mummy just redecorated with her friend Lawrence. He dresses a bit like a pirate." The way Beth said his name made it perfectly clear that she disapproved.

She talked me all the way through the ground floor but I heard nothing. Every new space we stepped into seemed grander and more opulent than the last. But the house felt cold to me, as if its heart had been buried deep under the shiny surfaces.

Beth seemed pleased to have my company and continued the tour to the upper floors. Beautiful bathrooms with unusual fittings looked more like museum showpieces than the rooms a family used on a day-to-day basis.

She hurried past one door without opening it.

I stopped. "And what's in there?"

"That's Mummy's room. I'm not allowed in there when she's asleep."

I checked my watch. "It's two in the afternoon."

"She has one of her heads."

Beth's room was on the top floor, at the back of the house. Just as I had expected, it was as oddly decorated as Beth herself. She threw herself onto her bed, and then peered under it for something, pulling it out and presenting it to me.

"What's this?"

"It's a gift. I made it for you."

I hoped she wasn't harbouring a crush on me. I opened the little blue box's lid tentatively and took out the tissue paper on top. Inside a papier-mâché figurine rested on more tissue.

"It's a merman," she said happily. "I'd already made the top half and then I heard Daddy say that he thought you looked fishy."

"He said that about me?"

"Don't take it personally. He doesn't like anyone."

"Sounds charming."

"My brother says he's a wanker," she said matter-of-factly. "What's a wanker?"

"You'll find out when you start dating," said an unexpected voice.

A woman who I assumed to be Beth's mother stood in the doorway, dressed only in a nightgown and clutching an empty crystal tumbler. She was everything Ruth wasn't. Ruth didn't wear jewellery to bed, and she certainly didn't drink alcohol during the day. This woman looked immaculate but dangerous.

"We're out of ice," she said testily. "Who on Earth are you?"

"Hello, Mrs. . .um. . .I'm Leven." I thrust my hand out just like Alex would and then snatched it back just as quickly.

She raised a pencilled eyebrow and pinned me in the blazing spotlight of her glare. "What sort of a name is that?"

"It's a nickname."

Her sudden disinterest was almost audible. "Sounds rather odd to me."

Beth broke the tension. "Leven loves his present, don't you?"

"Yeah," I agreed. "It's really great."

"Then expect to be inundated with them," said Beth's mother. "Everyone else loathes them. Who wants a lump of paper and glue as a gift? I'm going back to bed. Bethany, call your father and tell him to bring home some ice." She disappeared, albeit unsteadily, as quickly as she'd appeared.

"Your mum is-"

"A. Drunk. B. Horrible. C. A complete cow. My brother always goes for C." She paused. "So does Daddy, come to think of it."

"She doesn't need ice with a personality that cold. How old is she?"

"I have no idea. That's terrible isn't it? She's off to Switzerland soon for some serious work."

"And your brother, how old is he?"

"He's just turned sixteen. What school do you go to?"

"The Grammar."

"My brother went there but he's at Ellesmere now on a sports scholarship."

"I'm not really into sport. I'd rather draw."

"Me too!" She bounced from her bed and pulled out a large flat leather case. "This is my portfolio. Do you want to see it?" Before I could answer she was struggling with the zip in her eagerness to get it open.

Landscapes, fashion illustrations, and cartoons, all executed with exquisite attention to detail, spilled onto the floor.

I flicked through them, surprised. "You did all this?"

"Takes me ages. Mummy says I must get faster if I'm ever going to make a living at it. Lawrence thinks I could be the next Coco Chanel but I think he's just trying to curry favour with her."

Just as her mother had disappeared so did Beth, although I heard her pounding the stairs as she rushed downwards. I'd heard nothing, and wasn't sure whether or not I was supposed to follow her, but her chatter soon began and became louder as she made her way back to her room.

"-and his name's Leven but it's a nickname but I don't know what that means and he likes his gift and he met Mummy and survived and he loves my portfolio but I think he secretly thinks I traced some of it but he seems really, really nice!"

Behind her she dragged a boy bruised, grazed, and covered in mud.

But, despite that, he was unmistakably Shaun.

CHAPTER THREE
QUESTIONS

As soon as Beth said my name he must have known it was me but his attitude was as cold as his mother's. He barely acknowledged me at all as he spoke to his sister. "I'm guessing she's too pissed to have cooked. I'll grab a shower and make us something to eat. Put the kettle on, sis."

He stopped at her door and addressed me over his shoulder. "You staying?"

His obvious discomfort helped me decide. "I'd better get home."

"Suit yourself."

"No," Bethany wailed. "You've only just got here. Stay a bit longer."

Her pleading was so endearing I couldn't bear to disappoint her, even if it meant eating here in her room, away from him. "Well, if you don't mind."

Shaun grunted and left the room. The sound of running water soon followed.

Downstairs in the kitchen, I helped make three mugs of tea.

"No sugar for Shaun," she said, stopping my hand. "He's in training so he's only on good carbs and plenty of protein."

She seemed much older than fourteen.

Shaun reappeared, looking cleaner if no less battered, and started pulling ingredients out of the fridge. I watched him cook while Beth made small talk. Her brother responded in all the right places but with little emotion and I had no doubt that he was deeply perturbed by my presence.

Within minutes the most wonderful smell filled the kitchen, conveyed by the heat ascending from a wok.

I didn't speak until we were sitting around one end of a long dining table. "How are you settling in?"

His eyes didn't leave his plate. "This is the first time I've been home since we moved here."

"Oh right. Beth said you'd gone to a boarding school."

Beth interrupted. "How long have you been here, Leven?"

"I've lived here since I was nine."

Beth's mouth fell open. "Really? Shaun was five when we first moved to London for Daddy's job. Mummy was due to have me the day we moved. The doctor said that she was mad and that she mustn't want the baby if she was prepared to move house in her condition."

"I'm sure she wanted you," I said. I'd take Beth home myself if I could.

"I do wonder sometimes, the way she talks to me. Well, us. Do you mind not being wanted by your real mummy and daddy?" She suddenly burst into tears and I realised Shaun had kicked her under the table. She ran out of the room, leaving us alone.

He pushed his plate away. "Sorry. She's an idiot."

"She's just a kid." I kicked myself away from the table. "I'll go and check on her."

"She'll be fine. I've hit her harder than that before."

"She's your sister."

"She's a pain in the arse."

Not satisfied by his response, I found her in the small courtyard behind the house, crying quietly to herself as she rubbed her leg.

"I'm really sorry," she stammered. "I didn't mean to upset you."

I put my arm around her and patted her hair. She fell against me, sobbing freely now. "It's all right. I don't mind talking about it."

Shaun appeared bearing a bowl of ice cream and a bag of frozen peas.

Without speaking he handed her the bowl, crouched in front of her and applied the bag to her leg. She ate her ice cream with such a forlorn expression that I chuckled.

Red-eyed, she gazed up at me. "Is it very horrible, being adopted?"

"I'm fostered. I'm a bit too old for adoption now. It was horrible at first, being sent to live with all these strangers. I always felt like I had to do tricks to be accepted."

"Why have you been with more than one family?"

"I kept getting sent back."

"Why?"

"Beth," warned Shaun. "You're being very rude."

She offered me her ice cream as an apology but Shaun took the bowl and stood up.

"Who's still hungry?" He headed back into the kitchen and I helped Beth follow him.

Rummaging in the fridge, he pulled out more food. "I have to keep my food intake up while I'm training," he said, eager to explain that he wasn't just being greedy.

"Leven's not sporty," piped up Beth. "He prefers to draw, like me."

He tore off some cooked chicken and chewed it thoughtfully. "How about a swim?"

I went cold. "I've never been allowed to go near the water."

"Why not?"

"It's complicated."

"I could teach you."

"I don't even have a pair of trunks."

"I have a new pair you can have. Still got the tags on. Why not give it a go?"

Now he wanted me to stay? I asked myself why I was coming up with reasons not to. All I wanted to do was get some answers; ask him why he'd kissed me that night, and find out why he'd left. It was clear that he wasn't going to acknowledge that we already knew each other in front of his sister so I played along.

"Sure, why not? How far away is the pool from here?"

He grinned. "About twenty feet straight down. It's in the basement." It was his first smile since arriving home.

I'd expected plans to be made for later, not right now.

Beth groaned as her mother appeared looking no less testy but infinitely more sober. "Darling," the woman made it sound like an insult. "Come along. We have to go to your tiresome friend's equally tiresome mother's. . .thing."

"Ugh," Beth said, and then mother and daughter were gone to get Beth ready.

Shaun led me to his room, keeping the conversation light. I didn't know what to expect his bedroom to look like but I certainly didn't expect one wall of stacked firewood and furniture made from reclaimed materials.

"Do you like it?" He studied the room carefully. "It's the first time I've seen it."

"It's like a lodge."

"Is that good?" His uncertainty reassured me somehow. This was probably the first time he'd been in this room, his room, and he was nervous about my reaction to it. In a way, I felt like we were now on equal footing.

"Shaun, why did-"

"Later, OK? When we're alone."

"But-"

"Please?" He crossed the space between us and held the back of my head, holding his forehead against mine. "It's complicated."

I wanted to put my arms around him and kiss him but I knew he wouldn't want that, at least not right now, so I nodded and he set about finding me some trunks. He tossed them to me and I waited for him to leave, or at least turn his back but he stood, expectant.

Oh no. I wasn't ready for this. "Aren't you going to get changed too?"

"My costume is already on, see?" He pulled up his t-shirt and hiked down his shorts to demonstrate, revealing a solid torso as well as a band of brightly coloured fabric.

I decided that I'd probably changed in front of him before in a physical education class so I pulled off my jeans and underwear. Leaving my t-shirt on made me feel less naked.

He whistled. "Your girlfriend must be very happy."

I pulled on the trunks quickly, my face hot with embarrassment. "I don't have a girlfriend."

He took a step towards me. "Boyfriend?"

I shook my head and fell quiet as he reached out and pulled the waistband of my trunks out towards him then slid his hand down the front. What the hell was he doing? Talking was out of bounds but this was okay?

"You left the tag on," he smirked, snapping the plastic that tethered it to the fabric and threw it over his shoulder. "Ready?"

CHAPTER FOUR
LESSONS

Two flights of stairs later and we were in the basement. The pool was larger than I had expected. Shaun switched on the lights and then dimmed them until the illuminated pool was brighter than the room itself.

He yanked off his t-shirt and shorts and tossed them onto a wooden recliner.

"This is the shallow end, if you want to get in."

I took off my shirt and sat on the edge of the pool where he had indicated.

At the deep end he took up position and prepared to dive in.

I watched how his muscles moved across his ribcage as his arms extended upwards, how his legs flexed when he crouched, ready for his spring, then the perfect line of his body as he took off, arched forwards, and dove cleanly into the water.

I had expected Shaun to be clumsy in the water. I didn't know much about rugby but I knew what a typical player looked like, lumbering down the pitch like a juggernaut.

Shaun swam the length of the pool towards me and surfaced a few feet away, resting his weight on his arms in the shallow water. His shoulders bulged and I felt the familiar heat burn in my chest and work its way down.

"Get in then," he smiled, getting to his feet and holding out his hands.

The water cascaded down Shaun's body, and I felt my stomach twist with anxiety as I stood, desperate that he didn't notice what the heat had done to me. Suddenly unsteady, I waded into the water. It was warm and I was thankful for that.

To my relief something else had caught his eye. "What's that?" He nodded to my pendant.

My hand rose to my chest. "Ruth gave it to me."

"It looks like an arrowhead. What is it, flint?"

"Something like that. It's a sign of protection. Some local custom where's she's from." Since my adoption I had rid myself of my Scottish accent and felt no need to draw attention to my ancestry. School was all about fitting in.

Shaun waited patiently. He smiled as I moved towards him, not moving backwards into the deeper water until our hands met. He held onto me, his fingers intertwined with mine.

His instructions were gentle. "Relax your neck. Open out your shoulders. Breathe."

But my grip on him tightened. This was a big thing. As far as I could remember I had never been this close to this much water, let alone in it. My experience with the wet stuff extended only as far as baths and showers.

Shaun continued to encourage me. "Do you want to try putting your face in? That's good. Next time try breathing out under the water."

As I breathed out water rushed in and I took an involuntary breath. I came up fast, coughing hard.

"Sorry, sorry. Let's just stand here for a bit while you calm down. Christ, that pump is working overtime."

He was right; there was a definite current in the water around us.

I pinched my nose and concentrated on my breathing.

"Do you want to try floating? It's much easier than you think."

With his hand on my back, Shaun coaxed me off my feet and into his arms. I felt vulnerable then. This was more intimate than I thought it would be, alone with this stocky boy in the water.

"Now I want you to straighten out your body. Relax your neck again and let the water support your head. Don't worry, I've got you."

The sound cut in and out as the water lapped at my ears. Shaun's chest pressed against my side as I straightened out, his hands moving to support me between my shoulder blades and lower back.

"Relax, Leven. The water is your friend."

I floated on the surface and closed my eyes. A feeling of warmth and relaxation ballooned within me.

"Are you crying?"

My eyes snapped open and I felt hot tears streak down from the corners. I struggled to cover my face from embarrassment, but lashed out. Shaun cried out and let me go, clutching his face.

"Bloody hell!"

I disappeared below the water; my lungs filling with fluid. Coughing wildly didn't help; I was drowning. I bucked and kicked out, hoping to feel tile beneath me. I felt the current again, stronger this time. I was going to die in this pool, just as Ruth had always feared.

Then I felt hands under my arms and a sharp yank upwards. The cooler air meant that I was above water now, but I still coughed and gasped for air.

Shaun hauled me up to the steps at the shallow end and collapsed into a heap beside me, holding his face.

"What's wrong with you? You poked me in the bloody eye!"

"I'm sorry, OK?" I shouted, angry with embarrassment. "I freaked out."

"You're a nutter."

We sat on the steps, both breathing hard. I reached out to him. "Let me have a look."

He batted my hand away but I tried again, prising his hand from his face. His eye was pink and streaming, but I didn't see any damage.

"You'll live."

Shaun looked back at me, one eye open. "Until the day you drag me under."

"I told you I couldn't swim."

Beth stuck her head around the door, looking miserable. "We're off now. Play nicely, you two. Oh, and Shaun, remember that I found Leven first, okay? He's my friend."

He made a rude gesture in her direction then she was gone again.

"Shaun, can we talk-"

He stood up and reached out to me. "Come on. Let's try again."

I felt like I had no option but to accept that he wasn't ready to engage just yet. For now he was content with teaching me. I took his hands and prayed that I'd keep my cool as he walked slowly backwards so I only had to kick my legs.

Determined to impress him, I put all of my concentration into his instructions, putting my head in the water a few times to get the feel for it and practicing holding my breath with my face submerged.

After a few minutes he seemed happy with my progress.

"Do you want to give it a try without me? Just kick off and see how you get on. You'll be able to touch the bottom for ages yet, if you get into trouble."

Right then, this was it. I stood with my heels against the bottom steps and crouched down into a tuck. In one movement I put my head down into the water, pushed off from the step, and concentrated on swimming.

I felt the water split before me and rush down my sides as I kicked. Much faster than I'd expected my hands touched ceramic and I was moving so fast my head hit the tile too. A sharp pain travelled down my jarred neck and I clutched my head, breaking the surface.

"I'm so shit at this."

"Are you winding me up?" Shaun's voice sounded further away than I'd expected. "You swim like a fucking fish."

As I opened my eyes I discovered that instead of veering off to the side I'd hit my head on the opposite end of the pool.

Shaun stomped angrily out of the pool and wrapped a towel round his waist, yanking it tight. Scared at his reaction, I stayed in the water.

"You're honestly telling me that you've never been swimming in your life? Do me a favour. I'd kill to have your technique. You swam a length underwater and didn't even use your arms!"

"I swear to God I've never swum in my life." He didn't look convinced. "Maybe you're a better teacher than you thought?"

"The only thing I'm good at is rugby, trust me. I fuck everything else up."

We showered together in his parents' shower which was big enough for four people, let alone two. I wished I was built like Shaun, with proper muscle. Sure, I had a six pack but I felt skinny compared to him. He didn't speak to me or look in my direction.

Back in his room, he fired up his games console and slumped onto an oversized floor cushion, still irritated.

"Have you played this before? No? No doubt you'll be the best player ever. It's pretty simple, just shoot the zombies and don't shoot me. Go for head-shots if you can or shoot them in the knees and stamp on their heads."

I took the remote out of his hand and switched off the television, plunging the room into dim lamp-light.

"Why did you go, Shaun?"

He glared at me. "Do you want to stay over?"

Reaching out, I placed my hand on the side of his face. "Why did you go?"

"Go on, stay over."

"I've got school tomorrow, haven't you?"

"We get a longer Easter break than you. That's why I'm home. Tomorrow's Friday. You can afford to be tired on a Friday."

"Why would I be tired? Wouldn't we be sleeping?"

"Well, yeah. I mean, of course." He pulled my hand away but didn't let it go. "What did you think I meant?"

Frustrated that he still wouldn't talk about what had happened, I gathered my things to leave. "Thanks for having me. I had a really good time. Sorry about your eye."

Shaun followed me to his bedroom door. I opened it slowly. "I didn't hear your mum and Beth come back in. Do you think they're all right?"

"Mum probably got drunk, booked them a hotel room somewhere and passed out. Don't worry. Beth is a tough cookie. She's used to it."

The night was much colder than when I'd crossed the street earlier. I shivered as I ran up the stairs to my own bedroom.

I tried to sleep but I kept imagining that I was sitting on the edge of the pool, watching Shaun preparing to dive in. I admired his body as before and watched him dive in and swim towards me, but this time Shaun surfaced between my legs.

"Your girlfriend must be very happy," he said and I noticed that I wasn't wearing any trunks.

"I don't have a girlfriend."

"Boyfriend?"

"No."

"Then there's no one to mind me doing this," and Shaun's fingers closed around my-

My phone vibrated on the bedside table, startling me. I peered at the screen, my eyes adjusting to the brightness.

same time 2morro?

I stared at the message for a long time, my heart drumming in my chest. What did Shaun want? Was he laying in bed thinking about me? Was the swimming lesson an elaborate ruse to get me naked and for some physical contact? Would he have tried kissing me, or more, if I'd stayed over?

My fingers flashed across the buttons.

gr8 c u then

Thirty seconds later, my phone lit up again.

wish u cud av stayed 2nite but lukin 4ward 2 2morro nite m8

I didn't sleep a wink.

CHAPTER FIVE
PROTECTION

The next day at school was fuzzy. Geography blurred into Physics which blurred into English. The left side of my brain couldn't assimilate any new information because the right side was in overdrive, creating a million possible theories for Shaun's behaviour.

I practically ran home.

"Mum, is Alex in? Do you think he'd mind if I borrowed some of his aftershave?"

She hurried up the stairs after me. "Where are you going?"

"Beth's. I'm staying over tonight."

"You're what?!"

"No, no, it's not like that. You were right about her brother Shaun, we've made friends and he's invited me to stay over tonight. He's been giving me. . .. Is it OK?"

"It's wonderful. I'm so glad you've made friends. They seem like lovely children in spite of their mother."

I laughed, shocked. She rarely made snide remarks about anyone.

"Do you want some dinner before you go?"

"No thanks. I'm not hungry." I hadn't eaten all day. My stomach churned whenever I thought of Shaun.

Before I could react she had run to me and gathered me up in her arms, kissing my head. I felt her face turn wet.

"What's wrong?"

27

She let go of me and wiped her face. "You don't know, do you?"

I'd never seen her like this. "Know what?"

"You called me 'Mum'."

I had, when I first got home. It had come out so easily. And how she loved it. She dabbed her eyes and tried to control little involuntary sobs. I couldn't help but hug her and she held me so tightly that I thought she'd never let me go.

Now it was time for me to kiss her head. "You've been the best mum I could have wished for."

I shaved, showered, and dressed.

Ruth waved me off at the door, still sniffling, and it took all my powers of self-control not to run across the street.

Shaun answered the door, looking even paler than me. Dark circles lurked under his eyes, but how those green eyes danced.

"Hey you, come on in." He waved to Ruth and closed the door behind us. "Want a drink? My mouth feels like sandpaper."

"Have you got any cola?"

"You need a caffeine shot? I don't blame you. Think I'll have one too." Shaun got two cans from the fridge and set them down between us. "Didn't sleep?"

How could I tell Shaun I'd been up all night thinking about him? "Yeah, just um, you know. . .long day at school."

"Right," Shaun smiled, drawing the word out. "Long day."

Silence fell between us, finally pierced by the snap and hiss of him opening the cans.

"Where's Beth?"

"At a sleep-over. She wanted to stay here when she found out you were coming over but I persuaded Mother to accept the invitation. Beth's become quite a fan of you."

"And your mum and dad?"

"They've gone to Milan for the weekend. Some anniversary or something." Shaun rolled his eyes. "Like they need an excuse."

Another silence fell between us. I found the pattern on the marble work surface suddenly fascinating.

Shaun seemed awkward then. "Shall we go upstairs and get changed?"

"I've got my trunks on underneath."

A beat. "You mean my trunks." Was Shaun disappointed? Did he want to see me naked again? "Aren't they a bit tight? You barely fitted into them. I have some swim shorts that might be better for you. Why don't you try them on?"

I took a big gulp of cola and put the can down. It clattered as I did so, my hand shook so much.

Up in Shaun's room, the air seemed thick. As he took off his shirt his entire attitude from yesterday was gone. Now he seemed as nervous as I felt. He took the shorts out of a drawer and held them out.

"Here you go."

I took them. Shaun shifted his weight anxiously from one foot to the other.

"Aren't you going to change?"

"I've got my trunks on underneath too."

I eyed the bulge in Shaun's trousers. "Aren't they a bit tight?"

"You think so?"

"We're not really going swimming, are we?"

He rubbed the back of his neck. "We don't have to swim right now if you don't feel like it. Maybe later."

"Later? After what?" I was really pushing him now.

He turned his chin upwards and took a deep breath like he was just about to go under. "Um. . .video game?"

If this was going to happen I was going to have to make the first move. I shivered despite the room's warmth.

The kiss was tender, if not a little clumsy. As it deepened, Shaun's hands came up and rested on my waist. Teeth grazed lips, noses bumped, but it still felt good. Shaun tasted sweet like a vanilla bun. My hands came to life and travelled up Shaun's arms, feeling the solid, interlocking forms of bone and muscle. When my hands reached his shoulders, they reversed their journey.

Shaun pulled me closer to him and our hips met. I wondered if his flesh tasted as good as his mouth.

Leaning back from the waist, I tried untying Shaun's jogging bottoms but the knot was too tight. His hands closed over mine as he ducked his head down to look up at me, his eyes wide.

"Do you really want to?" But his hands were already on the knot, too. He worked it free.

I dropped a kiss onto his shoulder, across his collar bone, and down his chest. Lowering myself onto my knees, I kissed Shaun's abs and tugged his jogging pants down.

Shaun's trunks revealed the extent of his excitement and I was flattered that he wanted me so much.

I tugged on his waistband and he trembled at the touch. From the sticky mess within, Shaun had been excited for a long time. I took hold of it very gently and tasted the foreskin bunched at the tip. Shaun made a sound and I felt one of his hands in my hair. I looked up to see Shaun looking back down at me, his expression ecstatic.

Fluid leaked free as I pulled back his foreskin. The aroma intoxicated me and I wanted to taste it. I licked the tip and Shaun's cock bounced wildly. The taste exploded in my mouth, salt and sweet.

Shaun's grip on my head tightened and he pushed forwards a little. He tasted so good that I wanted to swallow him whole. My confidence grew and I sucked harder, my hands finding a natural resting place on Shaun's rock-hard arse.

A moment later his grip on my head tightened and he held me still while he rocked back and forth. He gazed down at me with a look that took me by surprise. Shaun's eyes had filled with tears. Then a shudder wracked his entire body and his head fell back.

His cum tasted as good as his mouth but this time the vanilla bun had been warmed through. Shaun cried out. The feeling must have been intense as his legs buckled. If I hadn't had such a tight hold on his buttocks I was sure that he would have fallen to his knees.

I swallowed hungrily while he gushed into my mouth. Looking up, I saw his chest and abs heave, his breathing laboured. Finally spent, he lifted me up for another kiss.

"Your turn," he grinned.

He walked me back to the edge of his bed and tugged my jeans down. I'd proved too much for Shaun's trunks to handle. When soft, I'd fitted snugly into them but now that I was hard I was too much to contain.

He pushed me back and I raised my hips so he could pull off my jeans and trunks, discarding them on the floor behind him. "Leven? They should have nick-named you Lucky."

Kneeling between my legs, he kissed my chest and smiled up at me wickedly before bringing one hand up to cup my balls. He tugged gently and squeezed them. My cock swayed between us, so hard that my foreskin peeled back of its own accord. Shaun dropped his head between my legs and licked my balls, looking up at me to gauge my reaction.

My whole body seemed to float upwards as if Shaun was still supporting me in the pool. He took my balls in his mouth and as he did so clear fluid oozed from my cock. Shaun licked it up, tracing it to its source, flicking his tongue over the tip.

His head bobbed as he started to suck. The sensation was better than anything I had imagined, better than a soapy fist in the shower, or a spit-covered palm. Shaun's tongue worked in circles with each rise and fall of his head.

"Stop or I'm going to come."

Shaun smiled up at me. His hand took over from his mouth as he spoke. "But I want you to come."

My hand closed over his. "I want this to last all night."

Laughing, Shaun sat back and displayed his cock which still stood proud. "Trust me, it will."

Not long after he resumed his work I felt a tightening in my balls. Shaun seemed to read the signs and worked harder. Just as I was about to come, Shaun swapped his hand for his mouth and sucked me until my orgasm ended. Smiling with delight, he crawled on top of me.

I saw thick white fluid behind his teeth and I frowned. "You didn't swallow?"

He shook his head.

"Why?"

He bent his head and kissed me. I tasted his sweetness again as well as my own. It felt wrong but I loved it anyway. He rocked back on his heels and reached behind to take hold of me again. "Round two?"

The remains of the evening and the entire night stretched out between us. We paused only to use the bathroom or get a drink but we were always within arm's reach of each other.

As mid-morning approached, Shaun lay next to me, lazily stroking my chest.

"I can't believe this is happening. You're so beautiful."

"You just like my cock," I laughed.

"Is that what you think?"

I shrugged. I'd given up trying to figure out what Shaun wanted. I didn't think he knew himself.

"Well I don't like your cock. No, I mean, I do, but that's not it. I really like you. You're so handsome it's unreal."

"Don't be daft. I wish I had a body like yours."

"You do, my body is yours."

"You know what I mean."

"You have a great physique. I didn't believe you when you said you didn't swim because you're built like a swimmer. Your school shirt was always too tight across the chest and shoulders."

Shaun's hand moved to my pendant. "What is this made of? It's heavy."

"It's iron."

"Shouldn't it be rusty?"

"It used to irritate my skin so Ruth, I mean Mum, lacquered it."

He dropped it back onto my skin, followed by a kiss. "That's a shame."

"Why?"

"If it rusted, it would be the same colour as my hair."

A door slammed downstairs followed by the sound of footsteps racing upwards.

"Fuck, it's Beth." Shaun leapt to his feet, threw my clothes at me, and pulled on his own jogging bottoms.

As he dove for the television, three things happened at once: the door swung open; the television screen lit up; and Shaun pulled up his trousers.

"Phew," Beth said, holding her nose. "It smells like boys in here."

She marched to the window and threw it open.

"The sleep-over was appalling. Can you believe that we had to have lights out at ten?" She plonked herself on the bed next to me. "I bet you two have been having fun all night."

The rest of the day was excruciating. Beth followed us everywhere and I had to restrain Shaun on more than one occasion when she drove herself between us.

"She's just a kid," I said. "Count yourself lucky that she doesn't know what's really going on. Besides, not being able to get my hands on you makes me want to get my hands on you even more."

"I want you so much," Shaun moaned. "I can't stand it."

"Then tonight will be amazing."

But after a sleepless night before, we both fell asleep soon after Beth insisted on watching a Disney movie.

Bleary-eyed, I woke to find them both asleep; Shaun curled up next to me, his arm across Beth, and resting on my thigh.

I lifted his arm off me and got up. Edging around Beth, I nudged Shaun's shoulder. He took some time to wake up but when he did, I put my finger to my lips and beckoned him upstairs.

Before his bedroom door was shut his mouth was on mine. We struggled with our clothes and then Shaun flung himself onto the bed.

And then my heart stopped as I realised that someone was in the room with us.

"GET THE HELL AWAY FROM MY SON!"

CHAPTER SIX
LOSS & GAIN

A hand grabbed my shoulder and flung me across the room. I cowered in the corner while the man advanced towards me, swearing loudly. I heard Shaun and Beth shouting for the man, their father, to stop but my clothes were hurled at me along with more abuse. Their mother stood in silence. My confusion froze me to the spot. It was the early hours of Sunday morning. What were their parents doing home? Hadn't Shaun said they were in Milan for the weekend?

"Daddy," screamed Beth. "Stop!"

"Beth, go to your room. No arguments, young lady. Bed. Now."

Leven nodded to her before she turned and left. Once her father heard her bedroom door close he rounded on me.

"If I was a fighting man, you'd be laid out on that floor. Your parents would be disgusted to know what you are."

"My parents love me and they'd be disgusted with you, not me."

"Then they're fools. They took scum like you into their home, showered you with love and affection and how do you repay them? You perform criminal acts, behave outrageously, and seduce my," he struggled with the words. "My son!"

"Dad-" Shaun began.

"You disgust me," his father continued. "You both disgust me."

Shaun tried to intervene but his father swatted him aside. Pure hatred filled me when I saw Shaun fall to the floor, his nose bloody.

The tirade of abuse continued as he dragged me down the stairs to the front door, finally pinning me to the wall by my throat.

"If I ever see you in this house again, or suspect that you have tried to contact my son, I will tell your parents what a disgusting, foul pervert they have brought into their home. No wonder your real parents got rid of you."

As he let me go, his hand caught in the cord that held my pendant around my neck. Angry, he yanked it away from me and the cord snapped.

The hatred spilled from me and I felt a throbbing in my temples. I raised my hand and pointed at him. "If you ever hurt me, or Shaun, again I will kill you."

He moved towards me, his face burning with rage, but suddenly stopped, clutching at his head. As he screamed with pain his wife ran to him but Shaun lay naked on the floor, looking as afraid as his father.

Amidst the chaos I pulled on my jeans and t-shirt, stuffing my socks and underwear into my pockets. I stole one more moment to look for my pendant but I couldn't see it.

I opened the front door and ran across the street, the screaming still ringing in my ears until I slammed my own front door shut behind me.

Thankfully neither Mum nor Alex were home. I slid down the wall, tears burning my cheeks. What the hell just happened? Had I killed him?

I climbed the stairs to my room but left the light off so I could watch Shaun's house. I didn't see any movement. I waited for half an hour but no one arrived or left. Surely if he was hurt they would have called an ambulance?

As I watched, it started to rain and the wind picked up, carrying debris from the park at the end of the street past the window. I looked up at a sky so polluted with light that the clouds were clearly visible. They moved but looked serene compared to the tops of the trees whipping in the air, shaken like I had been shaken by Shaun's father.

My thoughts turned to Mum and Alex. I was sure they would find out I was gay sooner or later. I didn't want to keep it a secret from them but I wanted to tell them when I was ready. But would I ever be ready?

I closed the curtains and crawled into bed. Using my phone's screen as a light I made a list of all the positive things that telling them would bring and then another of all the negative things. It took a long time to complete the lists because every sound in the street broke my concentration. My shoulders were tense and my legs started to cramp.

The list of negatives was longer.

I made a list of all the positive things that would come out of not telling them but they all seemed selfish. The list of negative things of not telling them wasn't as long as the other negative list but it weighed more heavily on my mind.

Concluding that I should do the right thing, I decided to tell them one by one, starting with Mum. I was sure she'd take the news best, and then we could tell Alex together. I hoped he would be as understanding. I just had to pick the right time.

A few months later I saw Beth briefly as she scurried from the house to the car. I froze, as did she, and then she gave me a short, secretive wave before I noticed her father's expression, angry then petrified, from the car window.

During that time my moods became erratic. I'd lose my temper over the slightest thing and it would take all my powers of concentration to calm down.

By the time my seventeenth birthday arrived I still hadn't seen Shaun.

"Happy birthday, darling," Mum cooed as she placed the most magnificent cake I'd ever seen in front of me.

My eyes filled with tears.

"Darling, whatever's the matter?"

I screwed up my eyes and shook my head before letting it fall into my hands, my shoulders heaving with sobs. "Mum, I'm. . .. Shaun and I. . .. Well, his dad found us. . .."

"I take it you weren't playing a board game, then?"

"No."

"Good-o," she said, her smile neutral. No, not neutral, restrained.

"I was expecting more than that."

"I love you?" She hugged me which made me cry.

"Don't you hate me?"

"Why should I?"

"Shaun's dad went mad. He kicked me out of their house and he called me terrible things."

"He is a horrible man, darling. Alex hasn't got a good thing to say about him. How is Shaun?"

"I don't know. I haven't heard from him. It's been nearly a year. I'm not allowed to see him or even call him."

She sat down beside me and held my hand. "I'm sure this will all blow over. Gerald, Shaun's father, is a very traditional man. He's a few years older than Alex and values were different then. At least one good thing has come out of this; Alex owes me fifty pounds."

"Why?"

Her mischievous grin blossomed. "I bet him you'd come out before we finished eating your birthday cake."

My mouth dropped open in horror. "How could you bet on something like that? It's sick."

Mum's expression hardened. For someone so positive this was a clear sign that she was as close to angry as she ever got. When Mum sighed, ordinary women would be screaming. "Would you rather I was packing your bags?" She held my face in her hands and wiped my tears away with her thumbs. "You are the most amazing thing that has ever happened to us. I wouldn't give you up for anything."

"But I've done such terrible things."

"I know, but this isn't one of them."

"I'm broken."

"You're not broken, darling. You're a bit chipped around the edges but you're not broken."

"What did I do to deserve you?"

Her smile was infectious. "Something wonderful, I expect. Now, come and open all these cards. Oh, here's Alex."

I balled my fists and steeled myself for what was about to come. With Mum by my side I was sure Alex would be okay but I took nothing for granted.

The door swung open and warm air swept into the room as Mum ran to meet Alex. Low whispers preceded a loud groan. Had she told him?

Alex stepped into the room and looked me up and down, a look of mild disgust on his face.

"It's true then? You're one of them?"

I gulped for air and nodded. Clearly Alex wasn't so keen on the idea of his foster son being gay.

Alex sighed and threw his coat and briefcase onto a chair.

"You've really disappointed me, Lev."

I nodded again, and shifted my weight uncomfortably, scared that Alex might go for me the way Gerald had. If he did I didn't want to hurt him too.

"I'm disappointed for two reasons. Number one, you've lost me fifty quid. Number two, because you've blown my news out of the water."

Mum looked as confused as me as he reached inside his suit jacket and tossed some papers at me.

I looked down at the papers in my lap but Mum reached them first, snatching them away from me.

She read quickly, her face a flurry of emotion. She dropped heavily into a chair.

"The adoption," she croaked, losing her composure. "It's granted. It's granted!"

She began to tremble, looking from Alex to me, and from me to Alex. Then she jumped to her feet, grabbed my hand and hauled me up as she launched herself at Alex.

"Oh, my boys. My boys! We're a proper family at last!"

But our family would be ripped apart in exactly one year.

CHAPTER SEVEN
ENDINGS

The topaz days we enjoyed for the next ten months turned obsidian.

Two months before my eighteenth birthday Mum fell ill. What had initially been diagnosed as Irritable Bowel Syndrome was, in fact, Cancer. A month later the correct diagnosis was made but by then it was too late.

As her pain increased so did the doses of morphine pumped into her failing body. She cried out often; incoherent phrases or, more distressing, obscenities. Swearing in our house was usually led by me, occasionally Dad, but never Mum.

On the eve of my birthday Dad called me out of a university open day and asked me to come home. When I barged through the front door I found him alone, polluted with worry.

"She has hours." It was all he could manage before what little light remained in his eyes collapsed in on itself.

We discussed what to do, agreeing to respect her wishes and keep her at home. She belonged with us. She deserved more than to die in some sterile, unfamiliar hospital bed. She should be at home, surrounded by the happy memories that we had created together. We held vigils at her bedside. I took the first, starting that evening.

I sat beside her bed and held her hand in mine as she slept. The woman sleeping in the bed was a pale imitation of the vital mother I loved so much. This time last year I had come out to her and she had made it a special thing. This time last year she had baked a cake; now she could barely open her eyes.

The thickness in my throat connected with the dull pain in my chest. Neither of us moved; my breath as shallow as hers.

As midnight passed, and my birthday began, Mum squeezed my hand and took her last breath. I was sure that she had held on by sheer force of will so she could welcome it with me. It would be the sort of thing that she'd do, I was sure of that. I'd have more birthdays but she, she was gone, and the slow decay of my heart began.

I stayed with her for another ten minutes, stroking her hand and witnessing her passing, before going to rouse Dad. But once I'd left her room I couldn't go back; she had been my mum before, now she was a body.

I went to my room when the doctor and funeral directors arrived, not wanting to remember anything but the peaceful look on her face. After so many days of seeing her face twisted in agony, she had seemed peaceful at last. I had no desire to see her body in a bag on a trolley, being manoeuvred downstairs and loaded into a vehicle by men she'd never known.

As they drove away, Dad knocked on my door and stepped in. He had changed from his robe into a shirt and jeans but the shirt was inside out and he was struggling with the buttons. His hands shook so much that I doubted he'd have been able to do them up anyway.

"She's gone," he mumbled.

I helped him put his shirt on properly. A private man, I rarely saw him undressed but now, even in the low lamplight in the room, my breath caught when I saw how much weight he'd lost. His gaunt face was nothing compared to the painful angles of his ribs and shoulder blades. He'd been working his usual long hours and sitting up with Mum most nights. I wondered how he'd done that before remembering that I'd laid awake night after night myself.

"She's gone," he repeated.

A cold sweat varnished my skin, and I sat down on my bed, suddenly unsteady. I could only nod.

"I'm going to go." his voice cracked. "Take care of the paperwork. Do you want to come?"

I shook my head.

"For me?"

I looked up at him. His hands fluttered at his sides like moths caught in a web. I rarely saw him without Mum; he was either at work, unseen, or at home with us both. A single tear spilled down his right cheek, his eyes wet with desperation. I stood and crossed to him, wrapping my arms around him as he buried his face in my neck.

"Oh God, son. What are we going to do without her?"

CHAPTER EIGHT
TRANSITION

Life after Mum's death became unrecognisable. Dad threw himself into work, rarely home in the daylight hours. I drifted, untethered from the real world. My plans for university shelved, I spent my days at home, feeling closer to Mum there and adopting her routine. If I couldn't have her here then I would remake myself as her, keeping her little rituals alive. But instead of time fulfilling its healing promise, it served only to illustrate how she had been the glue that kept our little family together. Kept me together. I knew that Dad loved me but he understood so little of what made me tick. Mum knew what I was thinking before I knew it myself.

"Maybe you'd like to come with me to the office?" Dad said one rare morning when I'd got up before him.

"What is it, Bring Your Child To Work day?" I sounded colder than I intended but I had tired of trying to tease a conversation out of him. Now that he'd tried I should have felt grateful but I only felt irritated. "It's okay; work is your therapy, not mine."

Dad looked down at the breakfast table, folding his cereal with his spoon. "It helps keep my mind off things."

"No." I stood up. "It helps keep your mind on other things."

Dad dropped his spoon into the bowl, and frowned. "Why are you so mad at me?"

"I could ask the same thing." I turned away and placed my hands flat out on the counter top.

"What are you talking about?" Dad sighed. "I love you."

"As much as Mum?"

I heard him stand and then a dull ring as he placed his bowl down beside me. He hugged me and kissed my forehead. It was an exact imitation of the way Mum kissed me when I was upset. "No one loves like she loved."

"That's what I'm worried about."

Saying nothing more, Dad gathered his things and left.

I tossed the bowls into the dishwasher and took a deep breath before letting it out in a long sigh. I'd almost achieved what I'd wanted – a family and boyfriend of my own. Just as I thought I had a boyfriend I lost him. And now, the family that I'd finally secured had been destroyed by the most evil disease imaginable. I was nine years old again. Lost and alone.

The doorbell rang. In no mood for visitors or cold callers I ignored it. I heard the letterbox open and something dropped lightly onto the doormat. I waited a moment and then went to see what it was.

A little blue box lay in the hallway. I picked it up and turned it over in my hands. There was no address, just my name; written beautifully in complex calligraphy. I opened the lid and gently removed the tissue paper.

Inside were two papier-mâché figurines. One an adult mermaid, the other a smaller merman. They interlocked in a hug, the mermaid kissing the merman's forehead.

I wrenched the front door open and a mess of silk clothes, muslin bags, and tousled hair launched towards me, nearly knocking me over.

"Lev! Oh Lev, it's so good to see you!" Beth cried into my neck as she held me tight. "I've missed you so much."

I hugged her for a long time, sobbing into her hair, then held her by the shoulders and straightened my arms to look at her; tanned, hair lightened by the sun, frame diminished by loss of puppy fat.

Looking down at her bags, I laughed. "What's all this stuff? Has Gerald kicked you out?"

"No, silly. I've just got back from school for the holidays and I had to see you before Mummy and Daddy." She dropped her bags in the hallway and ripped the silk scarf from her neck, before going into the lounge and collapsing onto the sofa.

"Won't they miss you?"

"If they do, they'll call. Oh, that reminds me," she switched her phone off. "Where's your dad?"

"Work. It takes his mind off things."

Beth's eyes roamed over me. She was still only sixteen but she looked more like a woman than other girls her age. "And what's taking your mind off things? You look exhausted. Not sleeping?"

"Not really."

She pulled me down onto the sofa with her and hugged me again. "You're skin and bone."

"Oh Beth, it's been so terrible without her. Dad is never here, and when he is he's so polite to me I could scream. It's like he doesn't even know me."

"Everyone grieves differently, sweetie."

"No, this is different. It's like we're both floating away from each other and I can't do anything about it. I want to talk to him about how I'm feeling but he avoids any conversation about Mum. It's like he's keeping something back from me but I can't think what."

"Just give him time, Lev. I'm sure he'll come back to you. Right now, you need to concentrate on yourself."

"How do you mean?"

Beth grimaced. "Let's start with a wash, shall we?" She grabbed my chin and scowled. "You could do with a shave, too. Then you're going to need a good, healthy meal and a nice, long walk."

"I don't go out much."

"Just as well, smelling like that," she laughed. "And we need to think about getting some meat back on your bones. You had such a great body."

I shrugged and ran a hand through my beard.

"What's the point?"

"The point is, sweetie, that you're never going to get a shag looking like a caveman." She stood and held out her hands to help me up.

"But Beth," I started to complain.

"Not another word. Bathroom!"

She stood in the doorway while I shaved. "You know, with a bit of work you'd make a great model."

I rolled my eyes. The man looking back at me in the mirror was in no state, or mood, to be any sort of model.

She ignored me. "I think that's why people are attracted to you – you seem completely unaware of how beautiful you are. One of the girls at school got scouted last month and she's convinced that she's a proper dog but the big fashion houses are going crazy for her."

She stepped out of the bathroom reluctantly as I slipped off my underwear and stepped into the shower. "I don't know why you're making me do this. My entire family has seen your willy."

It was the first time she'd mentioned Shaun, although indirectly. Even with the hot water pounding my body I felt a chill run through me. I finished my shower, dried myself, and wrapped a towel around my waist before opening the door.

"Why are you here, Beth?"

"Because you need a friend and I haven't been much of one."

"We haven't spoken in over two years and you've made no attempt to contact me. Why are you here?"

"How do you feel about a workout? Mummy's trainer is gorgeous. I think you'd make a good match."

"I'm not interested in him and you know why."

"Shaun isn't coming back."

"Why not? Where has he gone?"

"Please don't ask me to tell you. I can't say, but he isn't coming back. You have to face that."

"I'm tired of facing stuff. I've faced stuff all my life. Right now, I need a little dream time."

"Mummy's trainer is dreamy."

"Pack it in, okay? What's going on?"

She bit her bottom lip. "He's married."

"What?" I wiped wet hair from my brow, not really hearing her.

Her eyes darted nervously around the room then cleared her throat. "Shaun. Shaun is married. I didn't quite know how to tell you but I knew I had to."

My mouth dried out in a second and I struggled to speak. "When?"

"June. I'm so sorry."

I clenched my fists, feeling my nails dig into my skin. "I don't believe it. I don't fucking believe it!"

Beth squeezed her eyes shut and twisted her hands together. She started to babble. "His rugby scholarship didn't work out. Daddy was furious and demanded that he join the army. He met this girl and-"

I didn't want the details. I didn't care. "I've been locked away, grieving for Mum, pining for him, and he's off playing soldiers and fucking some bird."

"He's not happy." She looked scared of me, ready to run.

"Is that supposed to make me feel better? Knowing that the first guy I ever really cared about, and who I thought cared about me, has quite happily fucked off and left me behind? Where's my fucking wedding ring?"

Her face flushed. "You're talking about my brother."

"Your brother is a coward. Oh yeah, big hero on the rugby field but a pussy at home - terrified of Daddy. And as for that sack of shit, I hope he rots in hell. Shaun needs to grow a fucking backbone and face up to his sexuality. If he doesn't want me then fair enough but at least have the guts to accept the fact that he likes a cock in his gob."

"I can't listen to this. You're my best friend and he's my brother. I can't be in the middle."

"Best friend? We've been in each other's company for a couple of days and suddenly we're best friends? What kind of friend doesn't talk to her friend after seeing him thrown out of her house? What kind of friend does that? You are in the middle, Beth, but you chose not to take sides in this."

"Are you asking me to choose?" Her voice was angry now.

"You do what you have to do. I'm not going to ask you anything. I was fine before you and I'll be fine after you."

She gathered up her things and stormed towards the front door. "You can be such a. . .wanker! Go fuck yourself, Leven, but I guess that's all you'll ever get to do while you're locked up in this bloody tomb."

And she was gone.

We didn't speak for days. I holed myself away at home, refusing to go out or to see anyone. Not that anyone was breaking down the door to see me. I hadn't had a telephone call or email in months. Even cold callers had given up on me. Part of me was quite happy with that but the other part, the part that had been so happy to see Beth again after all this time, thumped dully in my gut.

I felt creepy doing it but I watched her house closely during that time, taking careful notice of when she jogged down the front steps and ran up the road towards the park.

Steeling myself one morning I pulled on my running gear and waited for her to leave. I gave her a five minute start and then followed in her direction.

I wasn't as fit as I had been and struggled to reach the top of the hill. As I gasped for breath, doubled over with my hands on my knees, I heard her voice beside me.

"I choose you."

I burst into tears and crouched down.

Beth patted my back. "We all let you down, Lev. I'm so sorry. I choose you."

I grabbed hold of her and crushed her into my chest, hoping that this one good thing would last.

But there was more news to come.

CHAPTER NINE
THE LETTER

Beth made a stand against her father. He didn't like it - I could hear him yelling from across the street — but he was no match for her. She had proven to be as fiery as her hair and as cutting as her mother. He finally conceded when Beth aced her final serve.

"Christ, it's not like he's ever going to be my boyfriend, is it?"

When she came skipping through my front door in her running gear she gave me a quick kiss on the cheek and launched herself onto the sofa as usual. I never knew why she did that; she was always back on her feet in moments.

I was so proud of her for standing up to him. She possessed all the courage that Shaun lacked. I leaned against the door frame and crossed my arms, smiling at her. "Now, come on. You would have liked me as a boyfriend, wouldn't you?"

She tried to keep a straight face but failed. "Ugh. You'd be terrible."

"How can you say such a thing?" I straightened, frowning.

She stood and walked over to me, biting her lower lip, and then placed her hands on my shoulders. "You're sexy, sweetie, but. . .."

"But what?"

"You're a mess." She shrugged, and bounded for the door, calling over her shoulder. "Come on, time for a run."

I sulked until we reached the park and then settled into the reassuring routine of both our route and our easy conversation.

That evening, Dad came home at a reasonable hour. It threw me completely but I managed to prepare a meal within thirty minutes of him appearing in the doorway like some ghostly apparition.

He prodded his food, and responded to my questions about his day with nods and shrugs, which made me increasingly frustrated. Why bother sitting down with me if he was going to remain silent? We'd both be better off if he just shut himself away in his study and ignored the situation instead of me. I'd adjusted to that. He'd adjusted to that. So why change things and make things uncomfortable? I'd had enough of coming away from our rare interactions feeling more miserable after than I was before. If I couldn't have a mother then at least let me have a father.

But during the silences I felt Dad's eyes on me. Whenever I looked back they'd flick back to his mash, pitted with absent-minded stabs from his fork.

"Potato isn't like fine wine, Dad. It doesn't get better with age." I felt bad as soon as I said it. He must need the love and reassurance I craved so badly but he refused to open up and let me in. My perseverance had turned to frustration.

Shifting in his seat, he swallowed, so thin now that his throat bobbed like an apple. "Did Mum ever talk to you about her family in Orkney?"

I tapped my lips with my fist as I thought, but all I could remember was the day Mum had given me my pendant.

"It's from your Auntie Margaret." She'd placed it around my neck with a flourish. "It's for your protection. You must never take it off."

"Protection from what?"

"If you don't take it off, you'll never have to find out." She smiled and kissed my forehead. "But I give it to you with one condition. You must promise me that you will never go into the water. No water of any kind. Do you promise me?"

I'd shivered at her words, recalling my nightmare of the dead dog. How could she have known? Had she guessed? "But-"

"Promise me. No pools, no rivers, no oceans. I lost my parents in the water, darling; I couldn't bear to lose you too."

At ten years old I was so concerned about what might be lurking out there, poised to strike the moment the pendant and I were separated, that I forgot to ask anything about its sender. Mum wanted me to stay away from water. I had no problem with that.

I wished I had the pendant now. Beth had searched her house several times but there was no sign of it. It had been a symbol of protection from the heritage that Mum and I shared. True, it was a heritage I had never known but that didn't alleviate my feelings of guilt at its loss. I broke my promise, swum with Shaun, lost the pendant, and now Mum was dead.

Dad prompted me. "Well, did she?"

I shook my head. "No, not really. Apart from her parents she only mentioned an aunt, and that was only once. I never thought to question her. Didn't you meet her family? I mean, you were married. What about the wedding?"

"It was just the two of us. She said that her surviving family would never approve of her marrying a Southerner so we did the whole eloping thing. She had as much flair for the dramatic as she did the romantic."

That sounded just like Mum. She had a way of getting what she wanted in the most difficult of circumstances and making the very best of it when she did so. Who would care that their families weren't there when the excitement of running away eclipsed any guilt she might have felt?

"Weren't Nan and Granddad mad that you married without them being there?"

Dad shrugged. "My dad was like your friend Shaun's. Once he realised that he couldn't control me he lost interest. He kicked me out at sixteen."

This was a revelation to me. On the few occasions that we had seen Dad's parents there was an omnipresent strain and I'd assumed it was some unresolved family argument but I'd never realised that Dad had been thrown out of his home. I felt closer to him for knowing this. We'd both been rejected by our families. How much worse had it been for Dad at his age? "What about Nan? Didn't she stop him?"

"She thought whatever she was told to." Dad had bored a tunnel through his mound of mash, lost in feelings that I felt guilty for having resurrected. "Would you like to meet them?"

"I have."

"Not my parents, Mum's family in Orkney."

My arms crossed, I leaned away from him. "Mum can't be replaced."

"I know, son. I know. I just thought. . .."

My first instinct was to get up and walk away but this was Dad's first real attempt at talking to me in the two months since Mum's death. If he had something on his mind I wanted him to feel comfortable enough to open up and talk. Really talk. Getting defensive wasn't going to do that. I gritted my teeth and sat back in as natural a position as I could muster but consciously thinking about being natural made it harder. I nodded, conveying my understanding, and we talked into the late evening, sharing stories of all the funny things Mum did, or said.

Finally, unable to ignore my tiredness, I bid Dad goodnight. "It'll be okay, Dad. You'll see."

His eyes shone with tears. "You think so?"

I hugged him tight and went to bed. Whether I believed it or not he needed to hear it.

The next morning, still in bed, I enjoyed the sun that streamed through the window and warmed my face. For the first time I hadn't woken from the nightmare. I'd still had it but the raw emotion was absent and I watched the events unfold with detachment. Feeling contented and rested, I enjoyed my slow, easy breathing, and the distant sound of children playing in the park. I stretched, catlike, and rolled over, my limbs loose.

Thinking about Mum, I decided that today would be a celebration of her memory rather than my usual moping about. I padded into my bathroom, showered and dressed, loving the feel of a fresh cotton shirt on my body and the hug of my favourite jeans. I opened my bedroom door, intending to pick up the paper, sit in the bay window, and watch the world go by. The park would be busy on a sunny weekend like this and I enjoyed seeing the families walk to and fro. In the mornings the children would be so excited they'd run ahead of their parents and in the afternoons they'd be slumped in their arms, fast asleep.

As I closed my bedroom door behind me, I startled Dad as he loitered on the landing, somehow managing to look crumpled despite wearing the white shirt I'd starched and ironed for him last weekend.

"It's Saturday," I said. "You're going to work?"

He clutched an envelope in his hand. The solemn look on his face signalled that this letter was urgent, important. Bad news.

I took a long, slow breath and cleared my throat but I couldn't talk. Dad pulled at his shirt and rubbed his head before he held the letter up to me.

Pressing a hand to my stomach, I stepped forward to take it. If I could have taken smaller steps I would have. Dad's behaviour was making me as agitated as he appeared.

As my eyes dropped to the envelope I saw my real name, Michael, my address scrawled across the front, and a jumble of stamps cowered in the upper right corner as if to get as far away from the inked words as possible. Dad made a sound as I turned it over and saw that it had been opened. He had opened it. He knew what it said.

It was obvious but I said it anyway. "You've read it?" I was on autopilot.

My eyes cut to his and he grimaced. "I'm sorry."

Before I could question him he hurried downstairs and left me to read it alone. What was so bad that he wouldn't hang around while I read it for myself? It must be really bad.

Back in my room, I sat on my bed and turned the letter over again to examine the writing. One hand had written my name using a black fountain pen, large, bold, and flamboyant. But another had written my address; small, scrappy, childlike letters. Who were these people?

Dad's behaviour was odd; there was no doubt about that. I felt genuinely scared of what the letter might contain. I reached for my phone and called Beth.

No answer.

Voice mail.

Fuck.

I threw the letter down and moved to the window to see if I could see any sign of Beth. Her moped was still there. I tapped the windowsill as I looked back at the letter on my bed. Despite the warm sun on my body, coldness settled upon me, my fingers almost numb. Rubbing them together, I snatched up the letter and ran downstairs. I heard Dad come out of the sitting room but I was already sprinting out the front door, jacket in one hand, letter in the other.

The street was empty of familiar faces, not that I knew many. I mulled over which direction to head in; the park to my right or the boutiques and coffee shops to my left? If Beth wasn't home she'd either be running or catching up with school-friends while they sipped coffee or shopped. As I was her only running partner I decided she'd only be a few streets away.

Praying that she wasn't just sleeping late, I considered which street to start my search for her. Apart from the park, I didn't venture far from home. More than one street in any direction and my heart would race, my breathing become shallow and laboured, and my vision blurred.

I swallowed down my apprehension and started walking to the end of the street, turning right and then left into the rows of boutiques and coffee shops.

I met no one's gaze, and went on my business with my head down, listening for Beth's voice. But despite my bowed head I knew exactly where everybody else was and what they were doing. My peripheral vision and hearing more than made up for my actual focus.

By the time I passed several shops with no sign of Beth I became aware of someone watching me. I looked up and saw someone move out of sight. A red-haired man sitting outside a coffee shop, I thought, but I couldn't be sure.

Shaun?

I crossed the street to where I'd seen the man but there was no sign of him. The empty table on the pavement marked the spot where he had been. I reached down to touch the half-drunk cup of coffee. It was still hot.

Unsettled, I returned home. I needed to grow some balls and read the letter myself. I wasn't a kid, too scared to open their exam results, I was a man.

As I turned back into my street, I saw the same man disappearing into Beth's house.

"Shaun!"

I broke into a sprint but the door slammed shut before I got a good look at who it was.

For the remainder of the day I sat alone in my room, the letter clutched in my hand, my eyes trained on Beth's house. Beth hadn't mentioned Shaun since she told me about his wedding. If he was home, I would wait all night for one more, one last, glimpse of him.

I wondered why if it was him he wouldn't have contacted me on his return before reminding myself that he hadn't contacted me at all. Perhaps his wife - wife! - was with him. Maybe he blamed me for his father finding us together. Maybe he was scared of me for what I'd done that night. God knows his dad was.

Thank heavens for Beth; without her I'd have no friends at all.

At just past midnight I saw her familiar shape tottering down the street, laden with shopping bags. Clearly Beth's day spent shopping had segued into a drinking session with her friends. She shouldn't be drinking at sixteen. Please God, I thought, don't let her end up like her drunken mother.

As she neared her house I hammered on my bedroom window to get her attention. She stopped and looked up and down the road like a lazy lighthouse, unable to identify the source of the sound.

I raced downstairs and into the street. As I reached her she dropped her bags and threw her arms around me.

"Levvy! Levvy-kins. My darling, I've had the most wonderful day. You should come out with me and the girls one night. They'd love y-"

I scooped up her bags in one hand and put my arm around her shoulder to guide her to my house. As she stumbled to keep up with me she chattered on about her day, what she'd bought, and the latest Primrose Hill gossip. In any other circumstance I'd be interested, living it with her, feeling less isolated than if I'd been left to my own devices, but right now I needed her strength and support.

Several black coffees later she was sober enough to realise the enormity of my reluctance to read the letter. She sat at the kitchen table, opposite me. I pushed it towards her but she didn't pick it up. She seemed as scared of its contents as I was.

"Your dad gave you this?"

I nodded.

"Have you spoken to him since?"

"No, I went out looking for you and when I got home he was out. He hasn't come back yet." As urgent as the letter was to me, I had another pressing concern. "Listen, Beth, earlier today I thought I saw-"

"Shaun's home."

I jumped to my feet. "I have to see him."

"Sit down, Lev."

"Why?"

She sighed as if she'd gone over this with me a hundred times. "He won't see you."

"Why not?"

"Why do you think? He doesn't want a scene."

Anger pushed against the boundary of my feelings. "Why are you protecting him? You chose me, remember?"

Beth laughed humourlessly. "I'm not protecting him. I'm protecting you. He doesn't want a scene because he's a coward. I don't want a scene because I don't want to see you get hurt."

"And if I want a scene? What about that?"

"I think you've had enough scenes to last you a lifetime, haven't you? Besides, this letter," she picked it up, "could prove to be a massive disappointment."

Her brow crumpled as she saw it had already been opened. The question formed on her face before she could ask me.

"Dad has read it." My answer was shaky.

"Didn't he tell you what it said?"

Sitting down, I shook my head then motioned for her to continue.

"Why didn't you just read it yourself? I'd be desperate to find out what it said."

"Please Beth. I can't handle any more bad news."

"You're becoming such a drama queen." She pulled a sheet of paper out of the envelope and unfolded it. What looked like a photograph, dropped face-down onto the table. I could just make out the brand printed diagonally across the back.

Beth pulled her legs up so her feet perched on the edge of her chair. Her knees rested on the table. She picked up the photograph and looked at it for a long time, looked at me, and then back at the photograph. Slowly, she put it down, face-down, on the table. Her eyes roamed across the page of the letter.

I watched her face for any flicker of emotion but it remained impassive and unreadable. When she finished the letter she put it on top of the photograph and pushed it towards me.

The tension was unbearable. I placed my hand on the letter but was still too scared to turn it over. "What?"

"Pour me a drink. A bloody big one."

CHAPTER TEN
THE ORCADIAN

The moment the man exploded through the doorway I wanted to run, and keep running, but fear anchored me to the spot.

After taking less than thirty seconds to read the letter it took me less than another five to accept its invitation. Now, two days later, I was here in the Orkneys and wondered if I should have taken longer to think about it.

Against the light flooding from the house the man was a black outline, a slab of threat, as tall and wide as the door itself. If he was anything like the wind in Orkney he wasn't going to bother to go around me and I, the immovable object, was already beaten into submission from the violent rain. One more step and I'd be trampled underfoot.

When he finally stopped in front of me my relief was palpable but it dissolved quickly when he grabbed me by my jacket and hauled me off my feet.

"Who ere ye?"

It took me a moment to process what he'd said. He had the thickest accent I'd heard during my journey here. My fellow passengers had tried to talk to me, once they'd finished staring, but I shrugged and pretended that I couldn't hear them over the whine of the transfer plane's engines. My mum's Orcadian accent had been extremely soft compared to the locals I'd met so far.

But it wasn't just their accents that confused me; I'd felt from the moment that I set foot on the island that the ocean tugged at my guts with an invisible force.

"Who ere ye?"

"You what?" I said immediately, an unconscious reaction as I translated what he'd said. It was a habit I'd grown into as a child, stalling for time when I'd done something wrong and needed to think up an excuse.

He lifted me higher until his face was level with mine. He remained silhouetted against the doorway so I couldn't make out his expression but his tone was unmistakable. As if talking to an imbecile, he repeated slowly, "Who ere ye?"

I opened my mouth but doubted that I'd be able to speak, from equal measures of fear and shock. Could this monstrous man be Mackay, my real father, who had invited me here? If he was he looked much bigger than his photo suggested.

He shook me for an answer. "Ere ye the beuy?"

Back in London I would have come back with something smart about being a man, not a boy. In my early teens I'd hung out with the wrong crowd long enough to hold my own but now, cold, wet and lonely, suspended in this brute's grip, my confidence melted away.

Mute, I nodded, and tried uselessly to pull his hands off me. I tasted a sudden salty bitterness but couldn't tell if I'd started crying or if it was the ocean spray whipped up from the waves that crashed somewhere out in the darkness. Right now all I wanted was to be back in London. I wasn't ready for this.

He set me down roughly. "Mackay's expectan ye." Fear loosened its grip on my guts. This man wasn't my father but that didn't stop his unrelenting attention from unsettling me.

Fresh barbs of rain shredded the last tatters of my patience. I should be welcomed as a guest, not assaulted and questioned like an intruder.

I puffed out my chest and set my chin high. I didn't feel confident so hoped I could fake it. "If I'm 'the boy' then I guess you're 'the help'?" The words left my lips less boldly than I'd have liked but I managed to get them out, and heard, over the storm.

This brute didn't look like any carer I'd ever seen but my father had written that his health was failing and someone looked after him.

The man drew himself up and I took an automatic step back, ready to flee if he lunged for me again, but he turned and opened the door, standing to the side so I'd have to squeeze pass him if I wanted to enter.

With his head turned towards me I detected one half of a sly smile on his face. "Hid's a bit blowy oot here. Ye'd better go in."

A bit blowy. At any moment I expected the house to be ripped from its foundations and he's calling it 'a bit blowy'?

I hesitated, half-expecting him to trip me as I passed him, but I shook the feeling off and stepped into the house. I fired a withering glare in his direction but underestimated his height and wasted the look on his collar bone.

I found myself in the kitchen and not the hallway as I'd expected. Blessed warmth radiated from an AGA on the far wall. I edged towards it like an acolyte, my hands raised in soporific adoration. The nearer I drew to the enamelled cooker the heavier my feet became.

He lobbed some fabric in my direction. "For yir her."

I looked down at a mangled tea towel so dirty that I resisted lobbing it right back at him but I was too polite to refuse. With one hand I rubbed it roughly over my head before unzipping my sodden jacket. His shadow loomed behind me and I felt him tugging at my shoulders, until he finally wrestled it off me.

The familiar sound of wood dragging against stone broke the silence and something hard nudged the back of my knees. He pushed me down into the chair he'd pulled up for me.

"Yir wet throo." No hint of concern presented itself in the statement so I didn't bother to respond. "Ah'm oot."

I must have misheard him. Surely, not even out here in the Orkneys, could Oot be a regular name. "Your name is Oot?"

"Nae. Me name," he strung the words out, "is Dom. Ah'm gaan oot." He remained out of sight. I heard what sounded like the rubbing of bricks on canvas and guessed he was already at the door.

"In this weather?" I realised to my horror that I sounded like Mum. "Where are you going?"

I got up to face him and my mouth fell open. He must have been six-foot-five with a smooth, olive tan and a jaw-line you could build a city on. And then there were his eyes, slate-grey and ominous. Stamped above each one was a thick, black brow, as if to certify the workmanship of the steel discs below.

He tucked a lock of wayward hair behind his ear and ran the same hand over his face. It rasped against his stubble.

My vanity urged me to run away again, to lock myself in a bathroom and not come out until I was washed and polished. But even then I doubted I could compare to him. Judging by the size of his shoulders and chest alone I needed six months in a gym, maybe more.

His breathing quickened as he studied me carefully but he remained silent. I vowed never to take my shirt off in front of him.

When he finally spoke he failed to keep the anger out of his voice. "Ah dinnae ansa tae thee."

"When will you be back?" I couldn't help it. Mum had always wanted to know where I was going and when I'd be back. Although it drove me up the wall I knew that she did it for the right reasons.

He tilted his head and his expression changed from defiance to surprise. "Ere ye a peedie simple, beuy? Ah'll see ye the morn's morneen. Dinnae disturb Mackay. He's no weel the night. Find yirself a room and do whit ye will."

A gust of freezing air whipped around me as he opened the door then slammed it shut behind him, leaving me cold and perplexed. Although I had understood that my father wasn't to be disturbed and that I should find a room, I'd need an interpreter for the rest.

Gathering up my things I explored my temporary home. The house was beautiful, the downstairs largely decorated in honey tones. I imagined bright coastal light flooding the rooms on sunny days. Everything seemed old but new at the same time. I recognised the furniture's classic design but also its pristine condition. Even the wallpaper, although old-fashioned, looked like it had just been hung; the colours vivid and bright. As I climbed the stairs I felt like I was on the set of a period drama and my clothes felt out of place among the antiques.

But there was no comfort here. Yes, the house was decorated with things that should have felt warm and inviting but it didn't. It felt like a forgotten place, never lived in by breathing, laughing, loving people.

I climbed the stairs and felt increasingly uncomfortable that each step took me closer to my father. I tried to imagine the hand that had written the letter inviting me here. I wasn't sure that I was ready to see him yet, if at all.

Doors flanked the landing on both sides and, at one end, light marked the edges of the only occupied room.

My father's room.

CHAPTER ELEVEN
EXPLORATION

My curiosity piqued, I tip-toed to the door and pressed my ear against it. I heard nothing, not even the sound of breathing.

Despite Dom's warning I put down my things and tried the handle. Locked. My hand shook so much that the door rattled in its frame. Anxious, I edged back down the landing and tried the four remaining doors. Two opened into bedrooms, another was locked and the last was the bathroom.

A tug on the pull cord illuminated the room. The strong, dark-green walls made the large, open room feel warm and cosy. Waist-high, vertical wood panelling drew my eyes down to a black-and-white tiled floor. A deep, roll-top, cast iron bath with clawed feet beckoned me to the other side.

I ran my hand along the smooth edge of the bath and smiled. My own bathroom at home was modern but it had no character. This bathroom looked like the magazine photos I'd pore over in a waiting room. Resisting the urge to run the water straight away I retrieved my things and set about choosing a bedroom.

One room faced inland and the other out to sea. To my mind there was no contest; I picked the room with the sea view and hoped that the weather would be better in the morning. I might not be allowed in the water but I still found it fascinating to watch.

The bed was a showy affair made from brass, elaborately dressed with drapes and lots of pillows. A round, marble-topped table served as a nightstand. On top of this table were a crocheted doily and a crystal lamp. A wooden dresser, also topped in marble, supported a tilting mirror. Drawers embellished with carvings sported ornate brass handles.

I looked at my reflection and confirmed the worst; I looked as terrible as I felt. Red welts circled my neck from where Dom had picked me up. Hopefully I wouldn't bruise. What had caused him to be so aggressive? How could my arrival trigger that sort of reaction?

With a deep sigh, I closed the curtains and turned on the bedside lamp. I switched off the main light, peeled off my wet clothes and emptied my case onto the bed.

The pained cry of an animal distracted me from sorting my clothes into the drawers and drew me to the window. I was surprised to hear anything over the wind that buffeted the house. Ignoring my nakedness, I pulled back the heavy velvet curtains and looked both left and right but saw nothing save for the uneven sheet of water running down the glass.

I closed the curtains again and finished my unpacking. As soon as I was dressed in something more appropriate for the weather, I went out to explore.

The rain had stopped but leaden clouds still edged across the sky. Mum had told me that during the summer months here the nights were never truly dark but the storm smothered the remaining light and made exploring difficult. I'd have to watch my step.

I checked my watch. Midnight.

I picked a path and followed it until it petered out close to the cliff's edge. To my right was the drop-off and beyond it the open sea.

A break in the cloud illuminated the muddy broth that churned and crashed against the beach below. My stomach tightened as I looked over the edge so I drew back, fearing I'd be picked up and flung into the waves.

I walked the other way, glancing back at the house. A dim red light from a second-floor room followed me like an eye. That must be my father's room. Perhaps the locked door led to another staircase?

Any island peaks had been weathered flat. Squat houses speckled the planed surface, hunkering down in the distance, as if scared to face the wrath of the howling wind that still raged around me. No living movement registered. Everything seemed to have found refuge where it could.

The ground hardened beneath my feet and became another path of sorts, the tough grass worn away by many feet. I followed and smiled when I finally saw the inviting glow of a pub, The Auld Hoose. Trust a pub to look like the only welcoming place here.

I loitered outside, unsure whether or not to go in, until the dropping temperature forced me to take shelter. I hoped the locals were friendlier than Dom because I wasn't in the mood for any more disappointment tonight.

But only wood-smoke greeted me as I stepped in. I flexed my stiff hands as I looked around. A slack-jawed woman stood behind the bar, staring at me with utter shock.

"Who are ye?"

"Hello." I didn't walk towards her but hovered by the entrance. She looked like she might scream at any moment. I had no idea what she was so frightened of and then remembered how late it was. I wasn't sure what the licensing laws were here but pubs weren't normally open this late. "I'm sorry. Are you closed?"

"Who are ye?"

"I'm Leven. I've just arrived."

Her hand flew to her mouth. "Are ye Mackay's beuy?"

Here we go. I nodded. "So I'm told."

She looked left and right at the five other people in the bar who watched me with equal astonishment. They were so quiet and still that I hadn't noticed them. To my left an old man sat by the fireplace while an old dog slept in his lap. The table of four men to my right realised they were staring, cast inscrutable looks at each other and then stared into their glasses instead.

It only seemed fair that I could ask a question of my own. "And you are?"

"Oh, I'm sorry. Where are me manners? I'm Maggs." She held out a podgy hand and her round face burst into a smile but, just as suddenly, she dropped her hand as her eyes filled with tears. "I'm very sorry for yer loss."

I was surprised that she knew about Mum but I didn't feel ready to ask her how she knew of her death. I still felt unsettled from Dom's reaction to my arrival and I didn't know who I could trust. "Thank you. Could I have a pint please?"

"He's got some manners then," one of the men chuckled. "Might be hope for him yet."

What the hell did that mean?

Maggs pulled the pint, placed it on a dog-eared bar towel and cast a look over me. "How's yer dad? We haven't seen him in a long time."

She asked about him so nicely that I knew she didn't like him at all and I wondered why. I gulped the pint down in a few seconds. "I haven't actually met him yet. Can I have another please?"

She pulled it. I drank it. Rinse and repeat. So far, so good. I figured that if I got drunk enough I'd pluck up the courage to ask about my father and, with a beer coat, I'd find my way back to the house without dying of exposure.

The men at the table looked amused at her obvious discomfort.

"And Dom?" she said. "How is he?"

Feeling reckless, I pulled down my collar to show her the welts on my neck.

"Dom did that? I don't believe it," she chuntered. Did this woman only do disbelief?

"You're joking, right? He's a madman. He talks gibberish."

She laughed incredulously. "His English is very good considering he. . .."

"He what?" It seemed there was more to both my father and Dom.

She ignored the question. "Ye must have scared him. Dom's the softest thing God put on this earth. I've never seen him raise his hand to anyone."

I felt a tiny spark of irritation at her attitude. As she continued to praise him the spark lit a low flame of anger. My right hand clenched around my glass as I tried to snuff the flame out. "Clearly you haven't seen him around many people."

"And is it any wonder, the way he's been treated?" Her entire head turned red as soon as she said it and I knew she was talking about Mackay. She busied herself by rubbing a cloth over a perfectly clean section of the bar and avoided further eye contact with me.

"Why? Did something happen between them?"

If she rubbed that counter any harder she'd take the varnish off it. "I've said too much."

"Beuy, Dom is the least of yer worries," a feeble voice chuckled to my left. It was the old boy by the fireplace.

"Tammie!" Maggs whirled to face him. "Don't ye be interfering now or I'll ask ye to settle yer tab."

"Oh shut up, woman." His milky eyes turned to me and he gave me a wide, toothless grin. "Buy me a whisky and I'll tell ye why folks around here aren't fond of yer father, although they might be too scared to admit it." He looked pointedly at Maggs.

Intrigued, I bought him his drink and settled into the carver chair beside him. The leather was old and dry, much like Tammie himself, but it was comfortable and warm from the fire.

He kicked off his shoes to reveal feet barely covered by ragged socks. The old dog on his lap barked softly in its sleep. "It boils down to this, beuy; folks on these islands have long memories."

"And I'm guessing not much else happens here to help them forget."

The joke wasn't lost on him but his little laugh turned into a larger cough. The dog slept through it. Tammie pulled a hankie from his pocket and dabbed his mouth with a trembling hand. "I'm sorry to say ye speak the truth but it goes back further than that. Something one of yer forefathers did still plays heavy on folk's minds to this day."

"That doesn't sound fair."

"Folks do forgive but yer father seems to be cut from the same cloth as the one that started all the trouble."

I took a gulp of my pint and didn't respond. I was in no place to defend a man I didn't know myself. Besides, I wanted to know as much about my family history as I could.

Tammie continued. "So back in eighteen fourteen some ferrylouper by the name of Mackay sets himself up on the island. Folks took an instant dislike to him-"

"Just because he was different?" Wait until they got a load of me.

"No beuy, no. Because he was a wrongdoer." He held up a fragile hand. "Let me finish. Mackay owned plenty of land but wasn't too keen on folks trampling over it to visit the standing stones scattered throughout. He decided to tear them down, every one, starting with the Odin Stone-"

"Odin? Isn't he a Viking god?"

Once more, Tammie's laugh turned into a chesty cough. "Got ourselves a genius here, Maggs. Yes, beuy. In that one act he goes from general dislike to absolute hatred."

"Because of a stone?"

"Not just any stone, the Odin Stone. Folks round here visited the stones for all sorts of reasons; some for celebration, some for ceremonies and some for altogether darker reasons. The Odin Stone was believed to be the most powerful one of them all."

The room felt a little colder as I absorbed what he was saying. "So what happened?"

"Within a day of the Odin Stone falling, some islanders tried to burn down his house and drive him away but he stood fast. Finally someone got the law involved and stopped him from destroying any more but the real damage was already done."

"Couldn't they rebuild it?"

Tammie shrugged. "How could they? The pieces were lost. There's the odd drunk who swears that his millstone is part of it but no one can prove anything."

"So that's why people don't like my father?"

"No, but the association doesn't do him any favours. No, yer father set his sights on the old lighthouse on the northern cliff. Told everyone he was restoring it. Word got out that he was turning it into apartments and the builders, all being local lads, walked out and left him with the shell. Then he got sick and we haven't seen him since." Tammie fixed me with his milky gaze. "I must say ye look well, considering."

"Considering what?"

He leaned towards me, his voice barely a whisper. "Considering yer father told us ye were dead."

CHAPTER TWELVE
DISMISSAL

Maggs appeared between us and snatched Tammie's glass from his clawed hand. "That's quite enough of that for one day, thank ye very much! Pay Tammie no attention, Leven. It's late and no doubt ye're keen to be getting home."

Tammie's dog woke up as they started bickering.

I'd stopped listening. I tried to process what Tammie had just said. Until recently, everyone had thought that I was dead.

Maggs was still talking. "- and he's on his way to fetch ye," she finished.

My attention shifted back from my thoughts. "Who?"

Tammie grinned at me again. He was enjoying this.

"Dom, of course. Ye looked a bit pale, beuy, so I thought ye'd be better off at home, not here listening to all this nonsense." She glared at Tammie before bustling her way back to the bar. "Oh, here he is now."

And there he stood, as gigantic and imposing as ever. To have arrived here so fast he must have been close by. Had he been watching me? He hovered in the doorway as I had done moments before. I was relieved that everyone stared at him for a change. One of the men at the table gave him a tentative wave which he acknowledged with a curt nod.

Tammie's dog growled at Dom and then pushed its head against its owner's hands, seeking comfort.

As he stroked the dog's greying head, Tammie sang softly.

"Ba, ba peerie t'ing, sleep a bonnie nappie; thoo'll sleep an' I will sing, makin' lassack happy. Ba, ba lammie noo, cuddle doon tae mammie; trowies canna tak' thoo, hushie ba lammie, hushie ba lammie, hushie ba. . .."

The song was familiar to me but I had no memory on which to attach either the lyric or the melody. The dog's eyes drooped and it was soon snoring again. My eyes felt heavy, too.

Maggs raised her eyebrows at Dom, her hands on her hips. When he didn't remove me fast enough for her liking she trundled over and pulled me up out of my chair. I dragged my feet like a reluctant child on its first day at school. She wanted me out of there. Fast. But why?

"I hope ye'll enjoy yer stay, beuy. If you need anything before that then I'm sure Dom can help ye. I've given him strict instructions not to let ye out of his sight until ye're safely on yer way home."

I looked up in time to catch a silent exchange between them before she squared up to him. "And Dom, ye be sure to speak yer best for Leven here, ye ken?"

He glared at me then cleared his throat. "Aye, Maggs, Ah'll try ma very best tae speak better."

We were hurried outside before I could even say goodnight to Tammie. I struggled to keep up with Dom as he strode off in the direction of the house.

"What happened?" he grumbled. "Maggs said ye looked scared."

"Like you care. The old boy was telling me stories."

"A great gappus, is Tammie. Pay him no attention."

"So where were you to have arrived so fast?"

A mist was coming in and in the faded light the house glowed like a candle in a frosted jar. Dom slowed a little and then stopped. By the time I caught up to him he stood motionless, looking at anything but me.

I searched his face. "Well?"

His steel eyes caught mine for a moment before he dropped his head but he still didn't reply.

Kicking a stone across the path I watched it skid and roll before it came to a stop against the side wall. Just how I felt;

sudden acceleration into this weirdness then - bam! - nothing. The only person that had told me anything so far was Tammie and I had been removed from his presence.

I pushed past Dom towards the house but stopped in front of the kitchen door. "Isn't there another way in?"

He gestured to my left. "Main door's roond there. Hasn't been used in years. Ah doubt Ah have the key."

I shrugged and shouldered the kitchen door open, the alcohol loosening my tongue. "No problem, I'm a back door kind of guy." I doubted he even knew what I meant. Gay guys from around here would probably have escaped on the first ferry to the mainland. In all my uncertainty I was sure of that at least.

Upstairs, I ran a bath and undressed quickly, eager to submerge myself into the steaming, foamy water. It felt so good to soak before I washed and shaved. I padded downstairs while I brushed my teeth and scanned the bookcase I'd noticed in the sitting room earlier. It took longer than planned so I swallowed mouthfuls of minty foam while I browsed.

A collection of pristine seventies paperbacks painted my father in a different light than I'd expected but the top shelves housed older, leather-bound tomes.

Several books on myths and legends caught my attention. As a kid, I'd loved the old movies about Greek heroes. On a cold, wet Sunday afternoon I'd wrap myself up and flick through the television channels until I found one to watch. I pulled a book about local legends off a shelf and climbed the stairs.

Getting into bed proved to be tricky. The sheet was fitted so tightly that, had they been any longer, I'd have bent my fingernails as I worked it loose enough to get in. As soon as my head hit the pillow my nose started to itch and I realised that the room needed a good dusting. I flipped the pillow over carefully then skimmed the stories in the book but my body had other ideas and I disappeared into sleep's shadows.

The sun burns down on me. The dog lies at my feet. The man lifts the dog into his arms. The dog's head slips from the man's arms and water pours out of its mouth. I can't take my eyes of the water trickling between the dead blades of grass. It is moving towards me like it's alive. I reach out. My hand looks different, blackened skin cracked like an old lady's heels. I touch the water and instantly it is gone. My hand looks normal again. I point it at the man. He clutches his chest and starts to scream.

But his scream turned out to be my own. I woke, my t-shirt soaked through with sweat and, as I lifted my head off the pillow, I felt more sweat trickle down the back of my neck. I tried to shake off the dream like I had on so many other nights. I lay still and concentrated on slowing my breathing.

Once my heart rate returned to normal I switched on the lamp and checked my watch. Four in the morning. I'd hardly slept at all. My head pounded and the room felt cold. I made a mental note to move the bed away from the exterior wall later.

I heard noises from downstairs, the rustle of a coat perhaps and then the kitchen door opened and closed. I pulled the bedspread tight around me and crossed to the window, sliding in behind the curtains.

A large figure hurried down the slope to the beach to the right of my bedroom window. It had to be Dom and I wondered where he was going, again, at this time of night.

Fully alert now, I decided to follow him. I threw on as many layers as I could manage and went out into the night. The bitter wind numbed my jaw, and I pulled my scarf up to ward off the ache that I knew it would turn into.

The slope was solid bedrock and I fell several times, too intent on not losing sight of Dom to pay much attention to my footing. Finally reaching the beach, I spotted him standing alone on the sand, a dozen feet from the tide mark.

As I approached, a wave raced towards him and he leaped backwards to avoid getting wet. I noticed how fast and graceful he was for his size but also that he moved like a man frightened not only of getting wet but of the water itself. His scared expression confirmed my suspicion.

He reacted to my arrival by turning his back on me and looking back out over the water.

I debated whether or not to keep walking and ignore him but he had seen me now. I had questions and was determined to get some answers.

"Mind if I join you?" I jammed my hands deeper into my pockets to keep them warm.

"Already here, aren't ye?" he said, his tone curt.

I forced a thin smile and tried to lighten my voice. "Didn't get off to a good start did we?"

"Nothing between us needs starting, beuy." His eyes never left the waves but the heavy lintel of his brow supported a furrowed forehead.

"Why are you out here so late?"

"Ye don't belong here. Go away."

"It's a public beach."

"Cheeky whalp. I could make ye disappear and no one would ever find ye, let alone care."

"Mackay might."

"Are ye as dumb as ye are ugly? Mackay thinks as much aboot ye as he does aboot me."

"You sound like a jilted boyfriend."

"What did ye say?" He took one step towards me and filled my field of vision.

"Well something weird is going on between the pair of you. Do you honestly expect me to believe that you're looking after him out of the goodness of your heart?"

As high as my voice had climbed, so his suddenly descended. "Ye're Mackay's beuy? His son?" I suspected the rumble of his last few words could be felt on the mainland.

The spark in my stomach, then the flame, returned. "Who the hell did you think I was?" I stood my ground and glared at him, desperate not to show how much he intimidated me.

He looked me up and down so slowly I wondered if he was simply taking the time to think through all the ways he was going to kick my arse. Then I noticed that his body shook. A slight tremble but noticeable. He didn't meet my gaze. "Ah think we're done here."

"I don't think-"

"Ah said we're done." Tension stiffened his body making every hair on mine turn spiky. I decided that Dom's bite may well be as bad as his bark and took a step backwards. I seemed to retreat from this guy more often than not.

"We'll see what my father has to say."

Spittle formed at the corners of his mouth. "Run tae yer father if ye want, he won't tell ye nothing whatsoever, then ye can get oot of ma sight, ye peedie bastard."

The flame exploded into fire. The speed of my punch surprised us both but he moved faster and stopped my incoming fist with his palm. He was so solid I felt like I'd punched concrete. Pain crackled through my forearm and up into my shoulder.

His eyes dilated - with what, fear? - but then narrowed as his huge fingers wrapped over mine, crushing them until my knees buckled with pain. I sank to the sand before he released me.

"Get away from me, his low growl quavered. "Now."

CHAPTER THIRTEEN
HEALING

Dom didn't need to tell me to get away from him a second time. He had frightened me but I had frightened myself more. I'd never swung the first punch before. I'd had a few fights back in my wayward days but I'd never started them. In fact I had been handy enough with my fists to be the one that finished them.

For now, all I wanted was to put distance between me and him. Physical pain might have ignited my sobs but it was the emotional pain that kept them fuelled. Despite the wind that cut across my path as I sprinted up the slope, adrenaline powered me through the effort.

Once inside the house I took the stairs two or three at a time and locked myself in my bedroom. I swallowed down my tears, sat cross-legged on the bed and pulled my injured hand out of my pocket. It felt so painful that I was reluctant to even look at it. When I did, the swollen mess made me sob anew and I fell back onto the dusty pillows. What the hell was I going to do? I pulled my phone out of my bag and tried to call Beth but there was no signal. I didn't remember seeing a phone in the house.

A sound above me caught my attention and I held my breath so I could listen. Maybe my father was awake? I jumped up, unlocked my door, and ran to his. I rattled the handle and banged on the door with my good hand before listening again. The sound stopped. I called out but there was no response. There had to be a phone here somewhere.

Downstairs, I searched the rest of the house to make sure that I hadn't overlooked a phone but to no avail. I would've gone back to the pub but the look between Maggs and Dom earlier unsettled me and I didn't feel like I could trust anyone except maybe Tammie.

I decided to bathe and bandage my hand and later that morning I would get help from someone else. Who – I didn't know, but somebody. I winced as the water ran over the split skin on my knuckles but the softest towel made a good, if bulky, dressing.

Back in bed, I switched off the lamp and closed my eyes but the painful throbbing in my hand distracted me. I tucked it under my other arm. The warmth and pressure soothed it just long enough for me to fall asleep.

I dreamed again. The dog, the man, the fear and anger. But this time the dog had been skinned. Then the dream flowed into something more immediate. I stood at the top of the cliff, overlooking the beach where Dom stood, watching the waves. A figure appeared from the water and said something inaudible to him after which Dom came back to the house and climbed the stairs to Mackay's room. Then the screaming started again.

Upright in bed, wet with sweat, my chest heaved with effort. Daylight crept around the edges of the heavy curtains. The house felt cold so I burrowed myself into the covers as far as I could, turning to my side and pulling my knees up to my chest. Late June shouldn't feel so bitter.

I jumped at a knock on the door, wincing when I moved my hand.

"Leven?" It was Dom. "Are ye awake?" His voice sounded softer but it was still gruff.

Tears rolled down my face. I wished he'd leave me alone. My hand felt worse than ever. Despite swallowing down one sob another escaped. I shifted my weight to push my face into the pillow. As I did so I caught my hand and gasped for breath as more pain stabbed through my fingers.

"Leven?" He knew I was awake but ignoring him. He must do. After a pause he said my name again and then his footsteps signalled his retreat downstairs.

Closing my eyes, I spent half an hour desperately trying to go back to sleep but, as the smell of cooking permeated the room, my empty stomach could bear no more.

After pulling on another pair of jogging bottoms and a sweatshirt, I shuffled out onto the freezing landing. Halfway down the stairs I turned back to put on two pairs of thick socks and my dressing gown.

Dom stood at the cooker, his back to me.

Assuming I'd get a frosty reception at best I said nothing and reached out to pull up a chair. Forgetting myself I used my crushed hand. "Shit!"

He yelped and a saucepan flew through the air followed by a loud clang as it struck the stone floor. "What do ye think ye're doing?" Dom roared, stepping back and crouching over something. He swore loudly and snatched his right hand back. "Fetch me the pipper." He reached out towards the table where a roughly-folded newspaper rested. I handed it to him, petrified that he might attack me before I remembered that I'd thrown the first punch last night. He scooped something up and tossed it into the bin. "There goes ma meat an' tattie pie."

"I'm sorry."

Despite wearing a thick jumper his impressive physique still showed through. As he stood at the sink I found myself watching the tectonic plates of his back shift while he scrubbed the pan.

"Ye scared me oot of ma wits."

He must have been browning off the meat for his pie. Rolled pastry languished on a floured block. So he could cook. Maybe he wasn't such a heathen after all.

My stomach growled, demanding food. "I'm really sorry. Is there anything to eat? I've had nothing since-"

"See for yerself." He cut me off without a glance in my direction. "Ah'm not here tae look after ye as well."

The spark ignited again inside me. "I don't need looking after."

He snorted. "Ye look like skin and bone tae me."

"I've got a swimmer's build." My voice rose too high to convince him.

He turned to face me. "Ye like tae swim, eh?" He looked interested in this fact and his gaze changed to focus on something between us, invisible to me. He relived a memory until a humourless chuckle brought him out of it.

"How old are ye?" He asked the question without looking at me. Instead, he pulled up the bottom of his jumper to examine it. Juices from the pan had spattered across the thick woollen fabric and he reached for a damp cloth to dab at the marks. My eyes were fixed on his taught, hard abdomen. Each segment was clearly defined and a thin trail of hair ran vertically along the middle. I would definitely not take my shirt off in front of him.

"I was eighteen in April." The smoky heat irritated my eyes until I clamped them shut and let the burning sensation pass. At least now he wouldn't catch me ogling him.

"Ye look older but ye still look like ye could do with some meat in yer belly."

"I'm pescetarian."

He laughed, a flurry of hoarse barks. Blunt white teeth flashed amongst his dark features. "Ye what?"

My skin prickled. "I don't eat meat."

"Yer a moppy!" Whatever a moppy was he found it hysterical. He clutched his sides and made more of it than I considered necessary. Conscious of a sudden blush my face burned even more. I should have been grateful to feel hot in this cold house. I moved closer to the AGA.

"Moppy?" I could only guess that this was some sort of local put-down.

"Ye ken. A moppy. Hops aboot. Eats carrots."

"Rabbit? Right. Got it." I rolled my eyes. As if a million vegetarians hadn't heard that as many times before. "No, I'm not vegetarian. I'm pescetarian."

His blank look disarmed me momentarily.

I sighed. "I don't eat meat but I do eat fish."

"Ah prefer fish maself." He opened the oven and pulled out a plate of sausage, bacon and congealed scrambled egg. "Guess ye won't be wanting this." He pulled up another chair and sat down, his thighs so big that they didn't fit under the table. It rested on them, wobbling as he tucked into the meal. He made a show of eating, a gleeful child who'd found a weak spot in another. I could only imagine the grief he'd be giving me about my diet despite his own preference for fish. I envied him though, being able to eat like that and still carry so little body fat. Watching him eat reminded me of a lion eating a deer. His ivory teeth tore through the meat and his powerful jaw ground it hungrily before his thick neck flexed with each swallow.

As he finished he shoved the plate towards me and gestured to the sink of soapy water.

I'd be damned if I was washing up on an empty stomach. I didn't take the plate but crossed my arms in defiance. Again the pain in my hand and arm made me wince. "I thought the housework was your job," I said through gritted teeth.

"Ah thought ye could help." His look hardened. "There's enough work here for two."

"I wouldn't want to put you out of a job. I mean, what would you do?"

"Get back tae ma own life, Ah hope."

"Which was?"

He paused. "Fishing."

I smiled and picked up the plate. I guessed that explained his physique. I'd watched enough documentaries to know that commercial fishing was physically demanding work. "So if I help with your work you'll split your wage?"

He shrugged. "Half of nothing is still nothing."

I blinked. "You don't get paid?"

Sitting back in his chair, which creaked ominously, he flicked a speck of bacon fat off the table then met my look of surprise with a defiant expression. "Ye ken a slave that does?"

I pondered this. Perhaps he only looked after my father in return for food and lodging. Out here it seemed like a suitable enough arrangement. Maggs had inferred he was badly treated but slave? "I thought-"

A short grunt sounded in his throat. "Ye thought wrong. Don't ken who's been telling ye what but ye don't ken the half of it. Maybe ye and Mackay need tae talk when he's feeling all right." Standing, he snatched the plate from me and stared me down until I looked away.

"Yes, I'd like to see my father now and find out what's really going on here." It was a half-lie. I didn't feel ready to see my father just yet so I intended to keep a low profile until I was. I'd almost ruined that by hammering on his door last night and reminded myself not to do that again. If Mackay was ill enough to stay out of my way but well enough to tell me what I needed to know then that was fine with me.

"What's that supposed tae mean?" Dom's brow bulged, a bumper on a truck. I imagined that he could toss me like a bull if I provoked him. Part of me wanted to try.

I pressed on. "Did something happen to you? Last night you seemed scared of the water."

"Ah'm not scared of anything." Dom's voice was low, but the phrase sounded like a mantra, not a statement.

"How did you come to care for my dad?"

"We have a contract. Nothing more."

"Contracts can be broken."

"Not this one, moppy. He's a stubborn old man. Ye'll never talk him intae letting me go."

"I'll give it a bloody good try."

Dom turned to me, his grey eyes electric. "Ah dinnae ken what tae make of ye. Ye seem tae think Ah'm after yer father's money but Ah've no need of it. There's only one thing Ah want from him."

Now we were getting somewhere. "What's that?"

"He took something from me. If ye help me tae get it back Ah promise ye'll never see me again. But Ah'm starting tae wonder why ye're here. From what folks are saying ye're dead tae him."

"I'm just here to meet my father," I said through gritted teeth.

"And that's all ye want? Then ye'll be gone?"

"Trust me; I'll paddle my own dinghy to get away from this shit-hole if I have to."

He seemed satisfied with that but his eyes still glittered dangerously. "Did Maggs say anything aboot me?" He tried to sound nonchalant but failed. His overly casual tone gave him away.

"Why? Something to hide?" I watched him as he opened the cupboard under the sink and retrieved a plastic bowl and a large metal pail. He set the bowl down in front of me, slightly to my right and poured fluid from the pail into it.

He reached over the table to take my injured hand which I instinctively withdrew.

"Ah won't hurt ye again. Ah promise." He lifted my forearm, pushed back my sleeve, and slowly lowered my hand into the water. I felt a fizzing that spread across my whole body. The water remained still and clear. My hand stopped throbbing and the pain disappeared.

I couldn't believe it. "No fu-"

"Ye swear tae much, moppy." He was firm but he didn't raise his voice.

Dom smiled grimly as I ducked my head in silent apology. Holding my arm up by the sleeve of my dressing gown, he swirled my hand in the fluid. The effect was hypnotic and I started to feel sleepy.

"Just let it work its magic," he said.

CHAPTER FOURTEEN
SURPRISE

After several minutes of bathing my hand Dom ran his palm over his face. "Water?"

"What about it?"

"Would ye like a drink of it?"

"Oh right. Yes please."

I slumped back in the chair and folded my arms across my chest as I tried to make sense of him. He didn't want to be here, and certainly not looking after anyone. He was moody and aggressive. Last night he'd crushed my hand and now he was bathing it. Maggs insisted that he was a gentle giant and now I'd seen a glimpse of that but I still felt wary of him. He was unpredictable.

He set a glass of water down and fell back into a chair, his limbs overflowing. "So, did she say anything aboot me tae ye?"

"Only that you're not as big a cun-"

"Language, moppy."

"Sorry. That you're not as big an idiot as you seem."

There was a knock at the door and Dom got up to answer it. I drained my glass while I listened to the incomprehensible exchange between him and the caller. Dom's natural accent remained impenetrable to me but the conversation sounded pleasant enough.

Dom returned with a small square package. At least it looked small in his hand. He placed it on the table between us. "It's yers."

I didn't reach for it at first but craned my neck so I could see the writing better. As soon as I saw Beth's carefully formed words I snatched it up and tore it open. It was kind of her to think of me and I was eager to see if she'd written me a letter along with whatever she'd sent. She must have sent it just after I'd left for it to get here so quickly.

My wish was granted and her letter connected me back to my life back home albeit briefly. It was almost as good as having her here. I read it twice and Dom didn't interrupt me. When I finally picked out a pale blue box, nestled in polystyrene chips, he cleared his throat.

"What is it?"

I laughed. "A house-warming gift."

Dom peered over the edge of the box as I lifted the lid and took out a papier-mâché figurine. I didn't know what it was at first; small, grey, bullet-shaped.

"It's a seal," Dom said. I wouldn't have paid any attention to his words had it not been for the fear and suspicion carved into each one.

In one quick movement he had snatched it from my grasp. How could a man so big move so fast?

"Why would someone send ye this?"

"Careful! Beth is my best friend and she makes them for me. I guess she thought it would be fitting seeing as I'm here."

"Where?"

"Where? Orkney. Where else?"

He looked confused then, not sure what to do.

I held out my hand. "Can I have it back?"

He didn't move. He might have been beautiful but he sure was maddening.

"Please, Dom?"

He gazed down at the little thing in his palm.

I sighed. "Fine, you can have it."

Looking like he was about to cry, he handed it back to me. "No, it's yers. Ah can't take it."

I thrust it straight back at him. "Then I'm giving it to you." I might not trust him yet but I got the distinct impression that Dom hadn't had much in life. If I could brighten it up a little with this then so be it.

The resulting smile practically bathed the room in the light I'd imagined on my arrival. Bright, bright sunlight. He extended his hand which I took, albeit with slight confusion. "It's time ye met yer father."

He tugged my hand and led me upstairs. The higher we climbed the softer his voice became. "Ah dinnae ken how long he'll be able tae talk but ye need tae see him."

The door at the end of the landing did indeed lead to another flight of steps that creaked ominously under our combined weight as we climbed.

We stopped on a tiny landing that barely had room for us both, let alone Dom.

"Are ye okay, moppy?" Dom looked concerned.

My mind turned to the size of this house compared to the others that cowered on the landscape. Why was this house so much bigger, especially as it seemed to be the closest to the shore? Building something this big on an island so ravaged by the weather seemed like an act of defiance itself.

Dom took the handle but didn't open it. "Are ye ready?"

I nodded but found myself gripping his arm. In the letter, Mackay had written that he'd tell me the truth about my past. What I really wanted to know was about my real mother.

Dom swung the door open and walked in. As he stepped to the side it took all my strength of will not to gasp at what I saw.

The man sleeping on the bed looked like a pale insect, gaunt and spindly, and nothing like the photo I'd received a few days ago. The bed which dwarfed him by comparison looked no bigger than my own at home and only served to illustrate how withered he was.

I took a tentative step towards him then looked back at Dom who gave me an encouraging nod, albeit accompanied by his usual frown.

My father woke as I approached him. His eyes were milky like Tammie's. He didn't see me at first and he blinked at the ceiling as if recalling a dream of his own. The tip of a small tongue darted around his lips and he swallowed hard before taking a shallow breath.

Dom whipped past me and offered up a small glass to my father's mouth before helping him up into a more upright position. He didn't appear to be able to sit up unaided so Dom stuffed pillows around his lower back.

Mackay noticed me then and lifted a pallid hand to beckon me over. "You're surprised at my appearance."

Mute once again, all I could do was nod.

"I'm not offended. I'm surprised too." He grimaced. "I'm quite ill."

His ill-health had caught me by surprise. "You should be in hospital."

"And be away from home?" he rasped. "No. I intend to die right here in this house."

I couldn't help but think of Mum.

Mackay coughed but it became a retch and again Dom tended to him. My father brought up a wad of brown phlegm. "But I doubt my health is of any concern to you."

"I'm here for the truth you offered me and then I'll be gone." It was as much as I could stand to say. I wanted to tell him that I had as little interest in him now as he had for me my whole life.

He shrugged his shoulders and I imagined the bones might puncture his parchment-thin skin. "You are welcome to stay here for as long as you wish. I don't expect you to care for me as Dom does but he might have some light duties to keep you occupied."

What the hell? "I'm here for some information, nothing else."

"Then you'll be staying for a while longer." He turned his head away from me.

"You said that you wanted me to know about her," I began but I knew this conversation was over when he didn't reply. I sprinted from the room and heard Dom following behind me but the narrow staircase slowed him down and I was at the kitchen door before he caught up with me.

"Don't go."

To my horror I burst into tears. "I hate it here."

He looked uncomfortable at my distress but patted my hair. "Ye're run ragged, moppy."

I wiped my face on my sleeve. He put his arm around me and the kind gesture made me sob harder.

"Ah'll run ye a bath."

He left me standing by the kitchen door. I slumped against it and cold air from outside tickled my heels as it blew in through the gap underneath. I knelt down to pull up my socks and my head thumped dully with an encroaching headache.

I heard the pipes in the walls shudder and then the sound of running water. The floorboards creaked under Dom's weight as he moved from room to room.

A bath would be good, I told myself. It would warm me through if nothing else. As I shambled up the stairs I heard Dom humming Tammie's lullaby. He swept past me, his massive arms overflowing with fresh towels.

He looked the other way as I undressed and lowered myself into the water. My skin tingled in exactly the same way as it had done when he bathed my hand. I pulled the mountain of bubbles around me, conscious of my inferior physique compared to his.

Dom sat on the dark wooden toilet lid and leaned forwards, elbows on his knees, his jumper straining around his shoulders and biceps. He said nothing at first which made me want to fill the silence but I resisted. Finally he rubbed his hands together and smiled sheepishly. "How is it?"

"So, so good. Thank you. What did you put in here, and the bowl?"

"It's a secret." He winked at me before turning solemn. "I'm sorry aboot yer father. He's a troubled man-"

"You don't need to make excuses for him."

Dom said nothing and silence grew between us again as I thought over our conversation at breakfast and my first encounter with my father.

"How would ye have felt if Ah'd just taken the gift yer friend sent tae ye?"

"I would have taken it back."

Dom laughed. "For a peedie beuy ye're awfully sure of yerself."

"What's mine belongs with me, no one else."

"And do ye think that applies tae everyone?"

The conversation had turned cryptic. "What are you getting at, Dom?"

He looked down and then up at the ceiling, as if he was wrestling with something. He took the seal figurine out of his pocket and looked at it before getting up and leaving the room. As the door closed behind him I shook my head in disbelief. When would I ever have a clear-cut conversation with someone here?

A moment later Dom returned and strode toward the bath, dropping to his knees beside it.

"Ah need yer help."

Mackay really did have something of Dom's and he wasn't going anywhere without it.

"This thing my father took from you. What is it?"

"Can't tell ye, moppy."

"It's not stolen, is it?"

His expression hardened. "Only from me."

I understood. Whatever it was, it had been forcibly taken from Dom and not offered freely.

"Are you sure it's here? Maybe he handed it off to someone else?"

He looked frustrated with me now and ran his hands through his inky hair. "Ah ken he has it."

"How can you be sure?"

"He kens Ah can't leave withoot it." His pleading look faded to black. "Ah don't want tae talk aboot it."

"Look, if I'm going to help you then you need to give me something to go on." I smacked the flat of my good hand on the water, frustrated. "I don't know, maybe I'm wasting my time."

He looked over his shoulder and then leaned in to whisper. "Ah'm sorry. Ah ken it's hard tae understand, but Ah can't tell ye too much."

"Too much? You're not telling me anything. Why?"

"Ah don't think ye would believe me. . .."

"And?"

His head fell. "Ah don't want it tae happen again."

"You think I'd take it, too?"

"It's-"

"Listen, I don't know what the hell went on between you two but I can promise you that I won't make the same mistake. Whatever this thing is, it's yours and not his. He took away my chance of a happy childhood and I can't get that back, but I'll be damned if I'll stand by and let him keep what's yours."

Raising his head, Dom reached into the bath. I flinched, not knowing what he was doing, and painfully aware of the intimacy of the situation, but he only took my hand. "He's a kind man, deep down."

I couldn't, wouldn't believe that. "I don't know what to say."

"Say nothing and do what ye promised. Ah want tae go home."

"That makes two of us."

Dom stood up and left. I sank back down into the water before realising that my cock was hard. For a moment I let my imagination play out what might have happened had Dom touched me, wondered how his mouth tasted, then shook the thought from my mind.

I was only here to uncover the truth.

CHAPTER FIFTEEN
THE IMPOSSIBLE

I rested for the remainder of the day. Dom cooked me fish for lunch and again for dinner. I'd never tasted food so fresh.

But later that night Dom left the house again and I decided to follow him. What was his fascination with the beach that he'd stand there night after night, gazing out at the sea?

But instead of making his way down the slope he walked along the cliff's edge, past the pub, to a part of the island I hadn't explored yet. I hung back as far as I could, conscious that there was little cover should he hear me over the breaking waves and turn to look behind him. I cursed the constant twilight this time of year brought and longed for the cover afforded by the relative darkness of a city night.

Dom leapt easily over a small wall and I noticed the canvas bag slung over his shoulder. He'd had that the night of my arrival. We were close enough inland for me to hear and recognise the same brushing sound it made in his hands. When I finally caught up I stayed behind the wall and used it to hide me.

At first I thought the building he walked towards was a larger croft house but it seemed too big compared to what I'd seen before. This building had two floors and was as large as several of the croft houses I'd seen so far. A smaller one-storey extension jutted out to the side but the bricks around the top had caved in and there was no roof. Most of the window panes were missing. No wonder Dom seemed so cool; the building was abandoned.

I ducked and scurried along the wall that ran around the building to get a better look into the extension, hoping the interior wall was also missing and would give me sight of what Dom was doing. Instead, I was surprised to see the remains of a waterwheel. The outer metal rims looked intact but most of the wooden slats were missing. Those that remained had turned green and white stains mottled their surfaces.

I heard Dom shoulder a door open so I hopped over the wall and looked for a window to observe him through.

He stood in front of a machine that I didn't recognise. The sides were made up of wooden slats but the frame they sat in had once been red. The colour was faded now but still stood out against the grey walls surrounding it.

Dom examined the machine with interest and then peered down the side of it that ran parallel with one wall. He reached out with one arm for something I couldn't see but then swore and stood back, his hands on his hips.

What was he trying to get?

As I wondered, Dom started to dismantle the machine using his bare hands. His muscles strained underneath his jumper as he did so. Gradually the wood splintered under his grip and gave way, revealing a row of large, circular stones propped up against the wall.

As soon as he was able to reach it, Dom pulled on the top surface of the second stone and rolled it towards him.

The surface of the stone was divided by deep grooves. Spreading away from these were smaller grooves arranged in eight repeating patterns. A large hole sat in the middle of what I now assumed was a millstone.

I felt a frown form across my brow. I'd seen no mill house on my father's land and certainly nothing visible from the house. What did Dom want with something like a millstone?

Once it was out in the open Dom examined it carefully before producing something from his pocket and skimming it along the edge of the stone. He examined the edge and smiled to himself. He ignored the other stones, each of which looked exactly the same to me.

Dom shoved the canvas bag into the back of his jeans and rubbed his hands together as if psyching himself up for something.

He knelt next to the stone and gripped it at its widest point, his knuckles turning white. Tucking his buttocks down until they skimmed the floor he began to stand. My mouth dropped open. Surely he didn't intend to pick the stone up?

If I'd thought that his thighs were big before my eyes widened as they exploded beneath their denim covering. The veins in his temple popped and every tendon in his neck strained as he gritted his teeth and continued to haul the stone upwards. It cleared the floor by six inches before Dom opened his mouth to roar into the twilight and, with a final, almighty push, raised the stone above his head.

I couldn't help but be moved by the sight of him standing like the ancient Greek titan Atlas, the weight of the stone as heavy as the world itself. If it wasn't for his heaving chest and the slight tremor in his mighty arms I would have mistaken him for a great bronze statue.

But the weight seemed too much for him. He held his breath and sank to his knees. The stone came to rest on his shoulder blades, his head dipped and his eyes closed. I had the sudden urge to leap through the glassless window and tear the stone away from him, lest he be harmed, but just as I was about to stand he whispered something under his breath and vanished.

I laughed as I fell backwards, the sound thunderous in the stillness of the mill house grounds. What the fuck had just happened? A rapid thumping began in my chest and my breath became shallow. I looked around for Dom but couldn't see him. The noise of my heart threatened to drown out the one overriding thought that popped into my mind. I had to get out of here.

I fell against the building and shook my head, trying to shrug off the dizziness but when I opened my eyes, my vision was still blurred. Cool air swept over me from the window and I lurched towards it.

I woke in darkness, my memories swimming up to paint in the broad strokes. Dom, stone, panic, pain. The pain remained. I lifted a hand to feel my body but my arm ached. A movement off to my left startled me and I cried out in surprise.

"Shh, Leven, it's OK." A familiar male voice whispered in the darkness. "Cover your eyes while I put a light on."

The light thundered in my head causing the pounding to intensify.

A cool hand felt my brow and adjusted my covers.

"Shaun? Is that you?"

"I bet you weren't expecting me."

"I thought you were gone."

"I'm back. It seems you're up to your old tricks. What happened? Did you freak out?"

"I've been having panic attacks since Mum. . .."

"I see. Well, you're hurt but you'll live. You went through a window. Lots of cuts to your arms and a bump on your head. No idea how you managed it though; it was thick glass. All that working out must be paying off."

"More trouble than it's worth, it seems."

Shaun laughed but he didn't smile. "Time for some painkillers. I've dressed your wounds, and you've a few stitches here and there."

"Where am I?"

Shaun smiled this time. "In your room. Sit up and take these."

"I feel terrible."

"Well, no surprises there. What happened?"

"I don't know. I've been getting anxious when I go out. I followed Dom to a mill house, he disappeared, and then I started to feel really dizzy."

"Disappeared? People don't disappear. Sounds like a panic attack to me. You need to learn to relax, mate."

I became aware of Shaun's hand on my thigh as he sat on the edge of the bed. Shaun followed my gaze to his hand but he left it there anyway.

"It's been a long time, hasn't it?"

Another memory came back to me. Painful and bitter. "How's the wife?"

Shaun's snatched his hand back and looked at the floor. I kept my eyes on him, trying to read his expression.

"You wouldn't understand."

"Try me."

"Dad packed me off to military school right after he found out about us. They always visited me after that. I was never allowed to come home. I was confused. Dad drummed it into me that it - you - was just a phase. When I met Charlotte I thought I was doing the right thing."

"For who?"

"For everyone."

"For me?"

"Especially you."

"How do you work that out?"

"Dad said you hated me. That Ruth and Alex were reconsidering your adoption. I had to stay away for your sake."

"Why didn't you write to me or try and contact me?"

"For the same reasons you didn't I expect."

"I didn't know where you were."

"Did you think I hated you?"

I nodded, mute.

"How could I ever hate you? You were my first."

"Really?"

"Really." He looked at me for a long time. "Can I kiss you? I'll be careful."

He didn't wait for an answer. He leaned in and brushed his lips against mine. Shaun tasted of vanilla sugar, just how I remembered him. Despite the shooting pains in my forearms, I raised my hands to hold Shaun's head, feeling the short brush of red hair, coarse in my fingers. Shaun had become much better at kissing, his mouth and tongue taking the lead. He leaned back, licked his lips, and smiled.

"I've missed you so much," I said.

"I've missed you too. I'm sorry I was such a coward. I was so scared that Dad might cause trouble for you with your parents. When I went away I prayed that you'd forget about me and that you'd find someone special. Has there been anyone?"

"No one." I stroked Shaun's face.

Shaun looked down at the bulge in his jogging bottoms and laughed. "Looks like he remembers you, too. Some things never change. I always had a hard-on around you."

I laughed and reached out to touch the mound of fabric, feeling the flesh underneath react to my touch. Shaun was very quiet now while he watched my hand working in his lap. After a moment, a damp patch soaked through to the surface of the thick jersey. I ran my thumb over it and brought it back to my lips.

"We have some unfinished business."

Shaun stood and shook himself free of his clothes, his fat cock jutting straight out. The tip glistened in the light and his cock bounced as he tore off his t-shirt.

"Is anyone here?" I was afraid of someone walking in on us. The shock of Shaun's dad discovering us still loomed in my mind.

Shaun shook his head and worked his shaft, swinging one leg up and across my chest, positioning his cock in front of my mouth. It smelled a day old, clean but fragrant. I licked the tip, tasting it, and realised that it tasted sweet, just like his mouth. He made a little sound as I took hold of his balls and felt their weight. They seemed bigger now. Everything about Shaun seemed bigger now. Years of training had solidified the muscle he sported when we were teenagers. He seemed more of a man than I'd ever felt.

I took a mouthful of his cock, running my tongue around the circumference of the tip, and let out a moan. The vibration caused a tremor in him and he pushed his cock deeper into my mouth. I looked up at him. He looked back down at me, his eyes riveted on the view. I wondered if any other men had sucked Shaun's cock since we had been caught so many years ago.

He twisted around and grabbed the shape of my cock through the blanket. The touch was enough to make me groan again. He clambered back on the bed and pulled the blanket back.

"Still no underwear, eh?" He smiled as my stiff prick lay between us, slick in its own goo.

He bent down and darted his tongue into the mess before he kissed me hard on the mouth.

"I really shouldn't be doing this with a patient," he purred, "but I'll make an exception for one as sexy as you. Now will you please fuck me?"

"You'll have to be on top."

"Just how I've thought about it." He winked and edged forward on the bed.

Once in position, he spat into his hand and coated my shaft with his spittle. The wet touch felt good and I couldn't help but jerk my hips off the bed a little.

Shaun smiled and raised an eyebrow.

"Sure you'll last?"

"As long as you, yeah."

Using more spit, he reached behind him and lubricated his hole before he lowered himself onto my shaft. We both sighed as the full insertion was complete. Shaun remained still apart from his cock which bounced wildly, triggering a tighter grip on my prod at the same time.

"I've thought about this for so fucking long."

I pulled myself up to rest on my elbows, ignoring the pain, and kissed him again. If Shaun started to ride me I didn't know how long I'd last so I enjoyed his mouth and the sensation of my cock inside him. Something that I didn't think would have ever happened and may not happen again. I had to enjoy every minute of this now.

The kiss was returned with passion. Locked together like this, our union so close, so intimate, seemed natural and inevitable. Shaun's legs bulged with the strain of holding him in position and started to tremble. He tipped his weight forwards to his knees. With a slow and steady rhythm, he started to ride me.

Shaun's cock was pointing upright now, flat against his stomach. I lay back, my hands behind my head, and enjoyed the view. He really had been taking care of himself, his body shaved except for a patch of dark red hair above that magnificent dick. His balls hung low and stuck briefly to my skin between strokes. Army dog tags hung in the deep valley of his chest, tapping against the hard flesh. His eyes never left mine and he smiled the whole time, big white teeth in contrast to his heavily freckled skin.

He swore and his cock erupted, squirting wildly across my stomach. The sudden clench of his arse around my dick took me by surprise and tipped me over an edge I hadn't realised I was so near. I gushed inside him, the thickening pump of my cock fighting the vice grip of Shaun's tight hole.

His mouth was on me again as we continued to come, hungry for something I had, almost devouring me as the orgasms gripped us both.

As the pumping slowed, our mouths disconnected, Shaun rocked back and then up, allowing my still-hard cock to slide out.

"Where did you learn to fuck like that?" I struggled to get my breath back.

"That was my first time." Shaun had a half-smile. "I told you your cock would be the first I ever took."

"That was years ago."

He laughed and kissed me. "I keep my promises."

"I don't know what to say."

"Say nothing and do what ye promised. Ah want tae go home."

"What?" I blinked hard and looked up into Shaun's eyes.

But they weren't Shaun's eyes. Two slate-grey eyes peered into mine.

It was Dom.

CHAPTER SIXTEEN
CONFUSION

"He doesn't belong here, Dom. Why don't ye see that?" The voice was female, pitched high with frustration.

"Ah don't belong here but here Ah am all the same." His voice rumbled at the opposite pitch to hers.

I opened my eyes. I was on the sofa in the lounge, draped in a blanket, a thick pillow behind my neck and shoulders. I swallowed and tasted blood in my parched mouth. I couldn't tell if it was early morning or late afternoon. The smell of freshly brewed coffee wafted into the room. I hadn't seen Dom drink anything but water so I assumed he knew this woman well enough to offer her a drink other than that.

I wasn't sure which memories were real and which were dreams. There was Dom, the mill house, his. . .disappearance, then Shaun.

My heart sank at the thought of him. I knew that he had been a dream.

Not wanting to alert Dom and his companion I stayed as still as possible while lifting the blanket. My head thumped and my limbs ached. I was naked except for the gauze which had been taped clumsily to patches of my skin. Blood had soaked through a number of them. The blanket was stuck to my parts of my stomach. With equal measures of horror and relief I realised that I'd had a wet dream.

"Ye don't understand the danger he's in," the woman pressed on. "If Tammie hadn't found him who knows what might have happened?"

"We're all in danger, Maggs."

So that's who it was. Maggs. What was she doing here?

"What do ye mean by that?"

Dom sounded frustrated. "Haven't ye looked outside? Do ye remember a Simmer Dim as bad as this?"

"Ye mean. . .?"

"Her power should be strong now, the seas should be calm, but this," I imagined him jutting a finger towards the window, "is his doing."

"Ye think she's dead?" There was fear in her voice.

"Ah can't say for sure but Ah think not. Ah'm sure Ah'd feel it if she was. But something is wrong, Ah know that much."

"Have ye. . .asked Mackay?" She sounded nervous now.

Dom grunted. "He tells me nothing. Ah'm expected tae do as Ah'm told withoot question."

"I could ask-"

"He trusts no one, not even the beuy."

"That doesn't surprise me."

"Why d'ye say that?"

"I can't tell ye, not yet, but there's a reason he was taken away. He must leave."

"No. Ah need him."

"Ye've told him?!"

"Not exactly. Ah can't find the words."

"I can't ever begin to understand what it's like for ye, Dom, to be here like this but ye have to think of the beuy. This is no time to be selfish."

I didn't need to see the fury on Dom's face. The sound of him trying to control his breathing and the snort through his nostrils was enough.

Silence followed, then Maggs' heavy sigh. I heard the kitchen door open before both the sound of the ocean and the freshness of the cool, salty air, rushed in.

"Please, Dom. Do what's right for him."

The door closed and the silence returned. I could only bear it for a moment before I raised my head to look into the kitchen. Dom sat at the table, his head in his hands.

"Dom?" My voice crackled as I called out his name.

He wiped his eyes with his sleeves before he stood up and walked in to kneel next to me but his thick lashes remained wet and his eyes were rimmed in red.

"Are ye all right, Moppy? Ye gave me a fright when Ah got home and ye were gone."

"You gave me a fright when you vanished." I tried to sit up but my movement caused my torn skin to stretch and burn with pain.

Dom placed one hand on my chest and pushed me gently back down into the cradle of the pillow. "Vanished?"

"I know what I saw. You picked up that stone and then you were gone."

"Ye must have dreamed it." He forced a smile that didn't reach his eyes and then patted my stomach. "Ye had quite a night." The silver sparkle flitted back into his eyes and I knew he was referring to the mess I'd made during the only thing that I was certain had been a dream. Shaun.

Mortified, I groaned. "Please tell me you and Maggs weren't here when-"

"She wasn't."

"But you?"

He didn't have to say a word. The look was enough. The same look of grinning triumph he'd given me while he'd eaten my breakfast a few days ago.

Covering my face with my palm, I squeezed my eyes shut. "I don't believe you saw that."

"Losh, it wasn't as loud as the other dreams ye've had."

"My nightmare? I've had that since I was a kid."

Dom's brow pressed down in thought. "Ah don't dream. At least not that Ah can remember."

"You don't even seem to sleep. You're out every night."

He attempted nonchalance and failed. "Why did ye follow me last night?"

"The same reason that anyone follows anyone. To see where they're going and what they're doing."

"And what did ye find oot?"

"Nothing I can be sure about. If anything I have more questions than-"

I felt the cold and smelled the salt before I heard the kitchen door burst back open. A flurry of small footsteps preceded Maggs' reappearance. She paused for a moment when she saw me awake but her urgency drove her into the room. "Dom, there's something ye should see."

Try as I might I couldn't jump up and follow them both outside as fast as I'd have liked. Each movement caused new shocks of pain to reverberate through me. By the time I'd wrapped the blanket around me, stood and steadied myself, both their voices had faded away. I shuffled to the kitchen door that still hung open, forgotten in their impatience to go outside. I rested against the door frame and squinted into the wind but saw neither of them.

Dom seemed to have interest in nothing but the object that my father had taken from him. If Maggs had come across it and showed him its location then maybe he'd take it and be on his way.

I wasn't sure how I felt about his potential departure. As much as I distrusted him I had to admit that he intrigued me. Dom was mean and aggressive, unpredictable and surly, but he was a beautiful creature too, like a bull penned in before a fight.

And I was increasingly certain that what I'd seen the night before was real. Dom had knelt on the floor of that mill-house, bearing an impossibly heavy weight, and mouthed a few words before he disappeared. I had to find out how he'd done it, where he'd gone, and why that stone was so important.

Mouth still dry, I started to make tea. I knew that a glass of water would have been better for me physically but I needed a sweet brew right now. As I sat at the table, flicking slowly through a newspaper full of names of people and places I didn't recognise, I heard Dom's heavy boots stomping towards the house. But there was something different about his stride; it was slower than usual and one boot dragged from time to time.

I started to ask if he was all right even before I saw his face and when I did I stopped asking. He had looked tired before but now he looked exhausted, his face drawn, his eyes even redder. He didn't acknowledge my unfinished question.

I asked a new one. "What happened?"

As I watched him retreat through the lounge and up the staircase I caught a few words. ". . .just need tae rest."

Upstairs, a key turned in a lock and a door opened and closed. Several muted steps followed and then nothing.

I turned back to the paper but didn't read. My mind filled with questions. The longer I stayed here the more questions I had. If anyone here had answers they were reluctant to share them with me but I wasn't going to stop asking them.

A movement to my left surprised me and, as the sharp intake of breath filled my lungs, my ribs protested.

Maggs stood in the kitchen doorway, her short round silhouette looking squat in its frame.

She looked surprised to see me sitting at the table. Her eyes darted from me to the mug of tea to the paper and back again. "Ye should be resting."

It wasn't an admonishment or order. The sincerity in her voice reassured me that Maggs wanted me gone for my own good.

"Why do you think I'm in danger?"

She wrung her hands, looking uncomfortable.

I sighed heavily and pushed the paper away from me. "Sit down, Maggs. I'll make a cup of tea."

As soon as I made to get up she hurried into the room to push me gently back down into my chair before leaping into a flurry of activity. "Don't be making me tea. I can do that perfectly well for maself." Her coat was off and her sleeves rolled up before I could protest so I sat back and watched her. The routine calmed her posture but her eyes still avoided mine. She appeared relieved to be occupied and the sound of her tea-making filled the yawning void of unanswered questions that stretched between us.

In a few minutes she had made her own tea and refilled mine. She sat to my right, facing the kitchen door.

I asked again. "Why do you think I'm in danger?"

"I'm starting to think that Dom was right. Maybe we're all in danger."

"But before he said that you were insistent that I was in danger. Just me. Why?"

"Yer mother told me that ye were." Avoiding my gaze again she dug at the surface of the painted mug with her thumbnail, as if to gouge off the glaze.

"My mother?"

"She'd appeared on Mackay's arm one day. He showed her off and rightly so. She was the loveliest thing to ever set foot on the island and more beautiful than the Simmer Dim itself. My father had lost a sheep and I was walking the shore, trying to find it, and there she was, exhausted, sobbing, and heavy with child. I knew there wasn't much time; that ye were on yer way, so I helped deliver ye right there on the beach. After ye were with us I went to bathe ye in the water but she grabbed me by my wrist. I've never known ferocity and strength like it for one so gentle and slight. She grabbed me by the wrist and told me to keep ye away from the water at all costs. I thought she was delirious, talking nonsense, but when I looked into her eyes I knew she believed it. She made me promise to protect ye."

"From water?"

"Yes, Michael."

The name, spoken so easily, startled me. "But I have showers, take baths, swim in pools. I'm fine."

"Ruth let ye swim?" The disapproval in her voice prodded my temper but it fizzled away when I realised that she'd used Mum's name.

"You knew my mum?"

"Oh ye poor, sweet beuy, of course I did." Maggs laughed and leaned forward to grasp my hand in hers. Who do ye think led her to ye?"

I shook my head, starting to feel sick. "I don't believe this."

"I'm the only one ye can believe, my beuy. No one else can tell ye what I know, even if they wanted to. There's a magic spell preventing it."

It hit me then, all the times people seemed on the brink of telling me what I wanted to know but shying away from the truth, always leaving me with more questions, more uncertainty, and more frustration. "So how would you know someone had cast a spell?"

"Because it was me that cast it."

CHAPTER SEVENTEEN
CRUELTY

"So you're a witch?"

Rammed into one corner of the sofa, curled into a ball, seemed to be the safest place to be while Maggs mopped up my vomit from the kitchen floor and opened the door and windows to allow the rooms downstairs to air. I pulled the blanket tighter around me, hoping that if I pulled tight enough it might keep my entire being from exploding. The answers I was finally getting made things seem foggier, not clearer.

She bustled into the room, wiping her chapped, red hands on her skirt. "No, not a witch. I'm not magical by nature so I don't go casting spells hither and thither. The toll on my body would be too great. Drink yer water, beuy."

She jutted her chin to the glass that sat on the table between us. I eyed it warily and she rolled her eyes.

"It's just water, Michael. Drink it."

"Will you please stop calling me that? My name is Leven."

"No, it's Michael. I named ye at yer mother's request. It was my grandfather's name and she liked it when I suggested it."

I snatched the glass up and drained it. "Listen to me. My name is Leven. I don't care what you called me when I was born or what's on my records. My name is Leven."

Her beady eyes surveyed me for a moment before she sat in the chair opposite me. "All right, beuy. All right. Leven it is."

"And why are you suddenly telling me the truth, assuming this is the truth? You couldn't wait to get rid of me the other night so why now?"

"The truth might be the only thing to convince ye to go back home."

"So where do we go from here? You're going to undo your spell and set me free on the island to find out what's going on?"

She cocked her head to one side. "How much has Dom told ye about himself?"

"Not much apart from he's some sort of prisoner or slave and that Mackay has something of his that's keeping him here."

"That's as much as he can tell ye. Have ye pushed him for more information?"

"Of course, but he says that he can't."

Maggs smiled triumphantly. "Ye see? He wants to tell ye but he can't."

"But what Dom wants to tell me isn't actually about me, is it?"

"No, but the spell isn't that specific. It's designed to keep the truth about this place from ye. Dom is a part of this place, that's all. If I could punch a hole in the spell and let Dom's truth be shared, would ye believe me and leave the island?"

"I think that you should answer a few more of my questions. How come I've been okay around water? You mentioned pools but I've been in swimming pools."

"It's living water that ye have to be kept from; anything that's connected to the sea. The continuous flow of river to ocean is forbidden for ye, even if ye're upstream."

"But why?"

"Something is waiting in the water for ye, beuy. Something ancient, something chaotic, something evil. Don't ye feel it when ye're here, so close to the sea?"

I thought back to the sensation I'd had travelling here, and again when I stood on the beach with Dom. I had felt something on both of those occasions but written it off as motion sickness.

"What happened to my mother?"

Maggs shrugged. "I honestly don't know. I left ye with her and went to find some clean water but when I returned only ye were there."

"So, you. . .?"

She smiled thinly. "I looked after ye as best I could but I'm not the mothering type. I'm clumsy at best. The only reason I haven't been fired from the pub for breaking so many glasses is that I own it myself."

"You gave me up for adoption?"

"Eventually, yes. I travelled down to London to keep ye as far from this place as I could but still keep you safe."

"There's a bloody great river in London, Maggs."

She chuckled then, the twinkle back in her eye. "I worried about that for a while but folk told me it was so dirty that no one in their right mind would ever dip their child's toe in it, let alone take them swimming."

"And my mum? You said you'd led her to me."

Maggs's smile turned sad then and she looked down at her hands as she spoke, her voice barely audible. "She was a good woman, Ruth. I've forgotten how many rituals I'd tried to see into yer future but nothing worked. All I could see was yer present and it broke my heart to see ye so alone and so angry at the world. As soon as I met her I knew she'd be the perfect mother for a young man like ye. She knew our folklore and customs, and longed for a baby from these islands, but the community was so small she soon realised that would never happen. She told me her story the night before she and Alex were due to move to London. They'd met and married while he'd been working here on one of those new-fangled energy-producing wave machines. I told her about ye, and where ye were."

My thoughts formed as I spoke them. "I know you think you saved me, and that you're still protecting me, but my whole life has been filled with questions that no one could ever answer. I have terrible dreams. I can do things that ordinary people can't do. I've grown up knowing that I'm different to everyone around me.

No one could tell me why. But you knew. You could have told me-"

"I couldn't. It wasn't safe."

"Safe? My life has been anything but safe. I've been farmed out to live with some despicable people, Maggs. I'd rather you'd brought me up and dropped me a few times than some of the things I've gone through at the hands of others."

She wrung her hands as she spoke. "I'm sorry, beuy. I thought it was for yer own good."

"And now I'm here anyway. Great plan, Maggs, really great plan."

"I see yer point. I'm sorry that I've interfered as I have. I thought I was doing the right thing. Ye didn't answer my question. If I can allow Dom to tell ye the truth about him, why he's really here, will ye leave?"

"I'll consider it."

She closed her eyes and her lips moved a little, as if rehearsing or recalling some half-remembered phrase. Then she opened her eyes and smiled at me. "It's done. I'll leave ye both to talk."

After gathering her things she left. I watched her shuffle off into the distance and then, confident the house was aired, closed the door and windows.

My body still ached from my injuries but I climbed the stairs to rest and wait for Dom to rise.

As I turned left to go into my room I noticed that Dom's bedroom door was slightly ajar. I hesitated at my own door and listened. His deep, slow breathing was all I could hear. I guessed that he was asleep. Slowly, I pushed against his door hoping that the hinges wouldn't squeak. I pushed a little too hard and to my horror the door swung inwards so fast that I was frightened it would bang against the wall and wake Dom.

I leaped forward and caught the handle just in time. To do so I crossed the threshold into his room.

Looking around, my jaw slackened.

CHAPTER EIGHTEEN
FRAGMENTS

Pinned to every surface of each wall was a newspaper cutting. Dom hadn't closed his curtains and enough light made it through the filthy nets that hung at his window to make those closest to me visible. Each one detailed the killing of one or more seals, the bodies of which had been washed, or in some cases dumped, onto the beach. In one story a naked man had been seen running from the scene. The police had investigated but found nothing to link the two incidents together.

Almost all of the yellowed cuttings blamed fishermen for the killings. The sharp decline in fish stocks meant greater competition and seals could be stopped with a bullet no matter how unethical it was.

There were too many articles to read. I made it across one half of the wall to my left when I heard a movement behind me. Startled, it turned to see Dom's face swathed in shadow, only the glint of his eyes signalling that he was awake and watching me.

"What is this?" I said.

He didn't answer. I took a step towards him, to ask again, but he pulled his knees up and hugged them to his chest as if afraid of me. I'd seen that reaction before in the children's home when a kid was scared to speak the truth. "Do ye remember being born?"

"Of course I don't." It might have been a lie. My earliest memory was fragmented. I recalled a body of water, stillness, raised voices, a terrible, spinning wall of waves, but that was all. It might have been some half-remembered dream. "Are you telling me that you do?"

He nodded, pulling his knees up tighter to his chest. It was the same position I had taken on the sofa an hour ago after emptying my stomach onto the kitchen floor. "Like ma brothers and sisters before me, Ah had two births; the first in water, the second on land."

I stood, speechless. Whatever Maggs had tried to do, it seemed to have worked. Lowering myself to the floor, I mirrored Dom's posture.

He watched me settle down to listen before he continued. "Ah don't remember ma first birth but ma second was. . .brutal. As Ah climbed out of the sea ma skin fell away. Ah became something else. A man. Ah couldn't understand with the feelings that rushed in tae take the place of what Ah now know tae be instincts. Ah howled like an abandoned pup and dove back intae the water tae escape them but the feelings followed me, crashing against my skull like waves on rock. My mother nudged me, eager that Ah return tae the land if only tae retrieve ma skin. Ah closed my throat tight and reached oot of the water, feeling for ma skin but the prickle of rough stone on these," he held out his right hand and flexed his fingers as if seeing them for the first time, "scared me."

For all his size and strength Dom looked like the most fragile of boys at the children's home, haunted by the memory of losing their parents or some recent experience at the hands of foster parents that no child deserved. I fought back the urge to fling myself across the room and hug him, not knowing how he'd react.

"Ah looked back at ma mother. She waited patiently, her expression unreadable tae ma new eyes. Ah turned back and pulled ma body oot of the water. Ah took a step, maybe two before Ah heard the sound of an engine behind me. Ah turned tae see a boat off shore. Fishermen. Ah paid them no notice. The sun came oot, felt so good on this skin. As Ah turned my head up tae the light Ah saw that the fishermen were almost upon us. The men warned me tae get away. Ah heard a shot and my youngest sister screamed, rolled over in the water, but then didn't move again. Her blood clouded the water aroond her. It was too late for the rest of them, too. Before my family could dive tae safety the rest of the men opened fire. All dead but me. Ah took a bullet meant for another but Ah lived." He rubbed his side unconsciously. "It was the only time that being a man wasn't a curse."

"What are you saying? You're a seal?"

"Ah'm a Selkie. When ma sealskin is removed Ah become a human of sorts."

"And Mackay, how did he come to take you?"

"He found me on the rocks, naked save for ma mother's blood. Ah'd pulled her body from the water. He got me clothes, food, but Ah wouldn't go with him. Ah slept on the rocks every night and he visited me every day until. . .."

I realised what had happened then. "He took your sealskin, didn't he?" I had spent so long thinking that no one's life was as bad as mine that I'd never considered that Dom's aggressive behaviour might be caused by his own rage against something that he couldn't control; the death of his family and the theft of his sealskin. I couldn't help but scoot across the floor, as close to Dom as I could get, before reaching up and touching his face, my palm resting below his ear as I ran my thumb along his cheekbone.

Dom's head hung low, his face shrouded in the darkness. It was getting colder. We sat in silence for several minutes, our breathing the only movement.

Eventually Dom spoke again. "When our sealskins are stolen, we can hear the sound of tearing in our souls. I can still hear it, feel it. It's like dying withoot the peace after."

"Why do you stand out on the beach every night?"

"Ah'm waiting."

"For what?"

"For peace but it doesn't come. Maybe if Ah wait long enough the sea will take me back before Ah forget ma old life."

"Do you have anyone left?"

He didn't speak and that was all the answer I needed. If there were more like him out there they weren't his family and I knew exactly how that felt.

He took my silence to mean something else. "Ye don't believe me? Ah understand." Taking me by the wrist he took my hand away from his face and turned away from me.

"Dom, where did you go last night when you disappeared?"

"Ah can't tell ye."

He didn't want to tell me. "You must be cold," I said, "and I'm uncomfortable. Let's go and find somewhere warmer. I don't know about you but I think better with a drink inside me."

"What do ye need tae think aboot?"

"How we're going to get your sealskin back."

Dom pulled an empty bottle of whiskey out from under the pile of rugs and looked guilty. "Ah drank the place dry weeks ago."

"Then we'll go to the pub. It'll be nice to have some normal people about us, especially now."

The pub was indeed warm. The smell of wood-smoke greeted us as we stepped in out of the cold. Dom's face glowed red and his hands looked stiff while he flexed them with a grimace, cupped them over his mouth, and blew hard.

"You got company, Dom?" said an unfamiliar barmaid, looking surprised.

"This is Leven. He's Mackay's beuy."

"Mackay has a son?!" She looked at me, unconvinced, and then remembered her job. "What will it be?"

"Two ales please. Ah'll be back in a moment," Dom said, and he disappeared through the door at the end of the bar.

She placed the glasses on a dog-eared bar towel and cast a look over me. "We haven't seen Mackay in here for a while now."

"He isn't well."

"Is that so?" She seemed suspicious now. "What's wrong with him?"

"I'm not sure. He doesn't talk about it."

"Is it AIDS?" The question shocked me and I became aware of the general sense of quiet in the pub. All eyes rested on me. "My uncle in Stromness had AIDS. Withered away he did. All chicken legs and a pot belly. Said it was his meds."

Dom reappeared at my side. "What's going on?"

My face finally felt hot. "She was asking about Mackay."

"That's kind of ye, Bessie. He sends his regards."

Dom tossed some coins on the bar, picked up the drinks, and steered me towards the fireplace.

"That woman is a wicked old cow," said Dom, falling into a chair that looked as old and fragile as Mackay himself. "She's been spreading rumours that he has some sort of disease caused by laying with men."

If it hadn't felt so awkward, I might have smiled at the quaint way Dom had put it.

"Did Mackay come here much?"

"He did once he got bored of me."

"Well you are pretty shitty company, Dom."

"Mind your language, lad," said a sturdy voice from behind me, causing me to spill my drink and swear again.

"Millie!" Dom stood and then lurched past me to hug an old woman so tightly that I thought she might disappear into his jumper entirely. I was surprised to feel jealousy towards her.

"Let go of me you big oaf," the old woman's muffled voice said. "You'll be the death of me."

"Ye've survived more than that," Dom chuckled, but he let the old woman go.

Millie staggered a little and then sat in a chair that Dom pulled up for her. She tugged her tatty woollen hat down over her ears, snatched my glass, and took a big swig, smacking her hairy lips together in satisfaction. "And you must be Leven. Maggs told me about you. She said you'll be leaving us soon."

"Don't believe everything you hear."

She winked at Dom. "I like this one already. He's got spirit."

"He's going tae help me, Millie." There was a solemnity to his voice that sealed the agreement between us and Millie was witness to it.

She raised her eyebrows and let out a long whistle. "You've got your work cut out for you, lad. Dom here has been waiting a long time. Let's hope that what you've agreed to won't end up being dangerous for your health."

"You know about him?"

"Of course I do. I was the first one he asked for help."

"But you didn't help him?"

"I tried, but. . .."
"But what?"
She shrugged. "It nearly killed me."

CHAPTER NINETEEN
TALL STORY

"What do you mean, it nearly killed you?"

Millie drained my glass and shuffled her chair closer to me. Dom leaned in to listen. "Mackay has friends in low places, if you catch my drift."

"Criminals?"

She looked at Dom and chuckled. "Something like that. They're undesirables but they're of a," she indicated Dom, "different variety."

"Selkies?"

Dom made a choking sound.

"Keep your voice down, lad. Not Selkies. Fin-men."

"What are they?"

"Sorcerers, shape shifters, thieves. They usually take us mortals but if you need something to be concealed you go to them."

"And you think Mackay gave them Dom's sealskin?"

"I'm sure of it."

"How so?"

"Because of what happened when I got close to it. It was last year, a few days before Christmas. A fine, clear night lit only by the stars as the moon was dark. I'd covered almost every square foot of the island and unless the Fin-men had hidden the skin in the ocean itself I was sure that I was almost upon it. I was on the northern coastal road when I saw something moving towards me.

It was big. Too big to be a man. When I realised what it was I knew it might be too late for me."

"You recognised it?"

"Only from the stories I'd heard growing up. My mother was a spiteful woman who frightened me with stories of it when I was bad. Nothing scares me like the Nuck."

"The Nuck?"

"An evil thing. You'd be forgiven for thinking it was a man on horseback but you'd be wrong. It's an unholy combination of fiend and steed. It can't be outrun and you'd be mad to turn your back on it."

"So what did you do?"

"Through my terror I remembered the one dim light of hope in my mother's stories. The Nuck can't cross fresh water."

I laughed. I had barely come to terms with the concept that Dom was a Selkie and now they expected me to swallow this? Maggs said she had only allowed Dom to tell me the unusual truth about himself. Millie must have lost her marbles and Dom was naive enough to believe her.

"Hang on, you're telling me that a creature that evil can't cross a puddle?"

Millie's expression turned thunderous. "This information might save your life, lad. If you've any hope of helping Dom you can be sure you'll need to face the Nuck."

She needed humouring. "Go on."

"I changed direction as close as I could to the stream that ran to my right. The Nuck changed direction too and sped up. Seeing my chance slipping away, I tore towards the running water as fast as I could. As soon as I thought I might make it I jumped with all my strength. It bellowed as I left the ground and I felt its breath, hot as fire, on my back. Then the pain blossomed on the back of my neck. I don't know if it caught a handful of my hair or set light to it but," she turned her head away from me and pulled up her hat to reveal a raw swathe of skin, "it won't heal."

I looked from Millie to Dom and back again. This felt like too much and the tenuous belief I had that Dom was a Selkie had been stretched tighter by this tale.

Millie tugged her hat back down into place and snorted. She knew I didn't believe her.

As Dom and I left the pub, I had to run to keep up with him. "Nice old girl, isn't she? Shame she's as mad as a brush."

"Ye don't believe her?" Dom stopped, surprised.

I almost ran into him. "I think she believes she saw something but how could something like that exist? It's crazy."

"These islands are ancient. Don't underestimate the power of the magic that lives here." Dom started to walk again, shaking his head.

"What? Where are you going?"

Dom continued to walk and said nothing.

I watched him go, raised my arms, and let them fall back to my sides. A smart retort evaded me so I ran after him. By the time I caught up, he'd reached a house with a stone wall. The place was deserted and in ruins. It felt colder here than anywhere else I'd been so far.

Dom scanned the outside of the house and then vaulted over the wall. He took a tentative step towards the structure and then turned back to face me.

"Seen a ghost?"

"Of course not."

"Just stand there and listen. Feel the energy in this place and Ah'll tell ye a story."

I fought the sudden urge to laugh but fell silent as Dom started to speak.

"Folk avoid this place now, especially at night. Years ago, a mother too full of grief tae let her two dead children go, secretly buried them in the garden. Folk got suspicious after a while and, unable to explain where they'd gone, she was arrested and taken away. Soon after, strange lights were seen in the garden. Witnesses were dismissed as drunks on account of this house being so near tae the pub but it soon became a place tae fear. Then police returned and started tae dig. They found the children's bodies and took them but the lights remained."

"Why are you telling me this?"

"Be quiet. Can ye feel them?"

"Don't be stupid. How-"

Dom closed his eyes. "Can ye feel them?"

I opened my mouth but stopped when something tickled my neck. Thinking it might be a loose curl I swept it away with my hand but the sensation moved down the centre of my back, like someone was tracing my spine with a cold finger tip.

Behind Dom, a cool blue light illuminated the front wall of the crumbling house. I watched it grow brighter then begin to move upwards. A tiny smile tilted Dom's mouth. He can't have known it was there but perhaps he felt it.

The light spread out and split in two. For a moment it looked like Dom had sprouted luminous wings but they continued to rise above his head and above the roof until they were out of view.

I looked back at Dom but he had disappeared from the spot where he had been standing. As I looked left and right someone grabbed me hard, wrenching me off my feet. I cried out and heard Dom's deep laugh as the big man swung me around and around.

"Let go, you bastard!"

Dom dumped me on the ground in a heap. I sprang to my feet and launched myself at him. He easily avoided me and laughed harder still. "Ye can't catch me, moppy."

That didn't stop me from trying again. This time I fell flat on my face. Dom reached down and pulled me up by the back of my jeans. I tried to punch him but he caught me by the wrist.

"Ye might want tae think twice aboot that," he warned me, his voice suddenly low.

I glared at him defiantly and tried to struggle but he held me fast, rendering me useless.

"Go on, I dare ye."

I went limp in his grip, furious but overcome with the realisation that if Dom could overpower me so easily then he'd pulverise me in a balls-out, man-to-man fight. Dangling in his paw seemed like a safer option after all.

He sensed the fight had gone from me and set me back down. Rubbing my wrists, I sat on the wall and he joined me. "What was that?"

"Ah told ye what it was."

"It can't be."

"Why not?"

"It just can't."

Dom chuckled and threw his arm around me, pulling me to him in a drunken gesture. I hadn't noticed him drink that much during Millie's story. "Wouldn't ye like tae see yer loved ones again, if they passed on, even if they were just a light in the sky?"

"They don't come back."

"That's not what Ah asked ye."

I remained silent as tears began to stream down my face. I folded up, my hands covering my scalp, huge sobs wracking my body until I gasped for air. Dom reached out and patted me awkwardly on the shoulder.

"Ah'm sorry. Didn't mean tae upset-"

I was on my feet again, angry. "They don't come back, okay? They don't. Sooner or later everyone fucks off and you're alone." And I was off, sprinting across the path and off into the darkness. Dom called after me but he was too far away for me to make his words out. Not that I cared. The sound of him running after me soon registered. He was making up the space between us fast. I was a great sprinter but Dom had a much longer stride.

His voice became clearer. "Careful! Ye're too close tae-"

Then the ground beneath me disappeared and I was flailing in the air, my legs kicking uselessly. Dom grabbed me in mid fall but that meant that he had launched himself into the air after me. Falling fast, he twisted us around before we hit the ground.

The impact was hard. My head snapped back onto Dom's face and I heard a crack followed by the feeling of warm fluid in my hair.

Even in the dimness I could see Dom's face was covered in blood. I touched the back of my head first to see if it was my scalp that was bleeding but my skin felt intact.

We had landed on a stretch of beach that I didn't recognise. Dom lay dazed on the sand, his eyes rolling in his head. I crouched down beside him and pushed him down as he tried to get up.

"Don't move. You could have concussion." I pulled off my shirt and dabbed Dom's face, avoiding his nose. "Sorry."

Dom grunted and snatched the shirt from me.

"Good runner, Ah'll give ye that."

Dom insisted on going back to the house. In the kitchen I tried to tend to Dom's face despite his protestations.

"Do it maself," he muttered, as I gently pressed a warm flannel to his face.

"It's the least I can do."

"Ye're more trouble than I thought."

"Serves you right for scaring the shit out of me."

"Ye don't belong here."

"Tell me about it. There, I think that's as good as it's going to get. I think your eyes are going to go black."

"Ma head is pounding. Ah'm going tae go tae bed."

"No. You shouldn't sleep yet."

"Ah'm fine."

"You don't know that."

"Keep yer voice down. Ye'll wake Mackay. At least turn the light oot."

Plunged into darkness, I sat down opposite Dom.

"Ah hate the smell of blood," Dom said.

I didn't know what to say so stated the obvious. "So, you're really alone?" I whispered in the dark.

Dom nodded silently.

I was so used to wearing my loss on my sleeve that the thought of telling Dom about my own life seemed vulgar. I tried to pitch it so I didn't sound like I was trying to outdo him.

"I killed a dog. I was only little but I remember bits of it. They told me that it had a heart attack as it ran towards me but I know it was me that killed it. I don't know how I did it but I can still hear its owner screaming."

"Ye dream aboot it. Ah hear ye at night."

"It's getting worse. Must be the sound of the waves. I thought it might help, you know, being here, but it wasn't such a great idea, I guess."

"Ye still have Mackay," Dom offered in consolation.

I shook my head. "It doesn't feel like we're even related. I've seen him once since I got here. I don't even know why he invited me. I grew up in a children's home, farmed out to family after family but I always ended back up there."

"Why?"

"No one ever told me but I know I had issues. I don't think I ever slept through an entire night without waking up screaming. The lack of sleep made me difficult. As I got older I tested everyone to their limits. Finally, I met Ruth and Alex and everything clicked. I couldn't believe my luck. They'd fostered ten kids before me. That's how I got my name. Alex used to call me 'Eleven' and it got shortened to 'Leven'."

"Would ye put the light back on, moppy?" Dom rubbed his nose tentatively and looked uncomfortable.

"What is it?"

He stood up. "Ye need tae come with me. Ah have tae give ye something."

"What?"

"Something important."

CHAPTER TWENTY
HIDEOUT

The sand whipped around us in the evening wind and the sharp grains stung my face as I hurried behind Dom's long stride. We arrived at a small opening in the cliff face and Dom pushed me through first. He struggled to fit between the jagged opening so I helped him through as best I could. It struck me then how warm Dom's hands were. I had shoved my hands deep into my pockets on the way here but they still felt frozen. Dom had done no such thing but his hands were still as warm as the kitchen stove.

I made myself as comfortable as I could considering I was cut and bruised.

Dom looked infinitely less comfortable than me, his size being the problem. It was impossible for us to fit into the tiny space without at least one part of us touching.

Dom's announcement had unsettled me. "What's going on?"

His big grey eyes turned toward the narrow mouth of the cave and he went silent.

"Dom?"

"The package that came for ye. . .."

"What about it?"

He reached into a crack in the cave wall and pulled something out of it. I couldn't see what it was; it was completely enclosed in his fist. "Ah found this in the bottom with that white stuff and Ah kept it for maself. Ah'm sorry."

He held out his fist and I tucked an open palm under it.

"Ah think ye might need it," he said as he dropped something heavy into my hand.

My hand closed around it and the shape felt familiar. There wasn't enough light in the cave to see it properly but I knew what it was.

The pendant.

Why hadn't Beth mentioned it in her letter? Dom said it had been in with the packing chips. Had someone in her family recognised it as mine, seen the parcel intended for me and tossed it in without her knowing? As my mind raced through the possibilities, I felt a burning sensation in my hand. One side of the pendant felt rough and my skin reacted to it.

A plaintive cry, like an animal in pain, rang out. I had heard the same cry the night of my arrival. It had drawn me to my bedroom window but I had seen nothing.

Dom cocked his head, momentarily distracted, and his massive body tensed. "We have tae get ye oot of here."

"Why?"

"Shh!" As his finger flew up to his mouth his voice dropped to a whisper. "No time tae explain. Come on."

Dom stooped and crossed to the cave's narrow entrance. Again I noticed how quickly he moved for such a big man. His thick brow furrowed in steady concentration as he scanned the beach. Dom held out his hand and beckoned me over. "Don't speak, don't even breathe. Ye must get away from this place. It's not safe now."

I nodded, muted by the warm palm he placed over my mouth. I hadn't seen anyone or anything on the island that looked as dangerous as Dom but even the big man looked nervous.

After one more glance outside, Dom squeezed back out of the cave onto the beach and pulled me through with a powerful tug.

"Run tae the house," Dom ordered.

But something else was wrong.

I looked up at the water, smooth as glass. The wind buffeted my face but the ocean remained unnaturally still. How could this be happening?

I heard movement behind me, and looked over my shoulder to see Dom sprinting across the sand, the uneven surface having no effect on him. Each footfall planted solidly into the sand as he rushed towards me, waving one hand in front of him.

"Get away from the water," Dom bellowed.

I heard movement again and looked back towards the water to see a dark figure rise from the surface, obsidian-black against the dim light reflected by the mirrored water. The figure seemed to suck light into itself. It started to move towards me, faster that I'd expected, and accelerated rapidly. Before I could even think about moving, one inky arm reached out to snatch me from the beach. As its fingers started to close in anticipation of my frozen state, I felt two large arms around me and I was wrenched back from the water. In an instant I was back at the edge of the beach. A shriek pierced the night, but there were two inhuman voices, not one. I cried out too, struggling to release myself from Dom's vice-like grip.

"Let go of me." I lashed out impotently, my fear giving me strength and my confusion sucking it away just as quickly.

"As soon as ye're safe," grunted Dom in reply. I could feel his warm breath in my hair as he pulled me close to him and stood up.

The world tilted as he tucked me effortlessly under his arm and began to run. In any other circumstance I'd have felt humiliated to be transported like this but my mental exhaustion finally won out over my body and I surrendered. Dom had saved me from whatever that thing was and I doubted it was so he could harm me himself.

The sea receded quickly as Dom accelerated and I began to recognise some of the landscape that whipped past us as he ran. We were headed back to the house. I relaxed as much as I could into Dom's grip, certain that he'd slow down soon but he showed no sign of stopping and I was surprised to see the house whip past us, a flash of the dimly-lit windows in the night. Just as I opened my mouth to speak everything went black and Dom skidded to a halt. We were inside. But inside what? Dom set me down gently and it took me a moment for my eyes to become accustomed to the darkness. I reached out and my hands met a large chunk of crispy matter, its texture vaguely familiar. Hay.

"We're in a barn?"

"Catch yer breath for a moment," said Dom, an unusual softness in his voice. "Ah've a feeling it's going tae be a long night."

Grateful for the pause, I slumped onto a bale swathed in waxy fabric, the unusual texture stimulating my senses as I splayed my fingers out, seeking enough traction to help me sit upright. Dom placed a large palm on my chest and pushed me slowly back down, just as he had before when I had woken on the living room sofa.

I lay in the dark, Dom's hand still on my chest. The warmth from the big man's hand spread through me and my breathing started to slow. I rested my cold hands on Dom's and the warmth spread through them too. Dom sat perpendicular to me, his head tilted up towards the enormous beams floating above us.

This time, when I tried to sit up, he let me. I kept behind him, sitting at right angles to the expanse of his back.

"What's happening?" I whispered the words as much to myself as to him.

"Ah'm not sure, moppy." His resigned tone offered me no comfort. I'd hoped that if he was what he said he was then he'd have some insight into the madness of the past few days.

"I feel like I'm going mad." My hands found their way up into my hair, rubbing my scalp before the balls of my hands found a resting place in the sockets of my eyes. Bright flashes popped behind my eyelids and then eased into shimmering clouds.

"The world's going mad, beuy."

"I thought my world had ended when Ruth died and then I got here."

"It's ma world that's going mad, not yers."

"Your world?"

Dom got up, crossed to the barn door, and opened it. A slice of moonlight illuminated one half of his face. I got up and crossed over to him, taking in a breath to speak but his hand came up to silence me. I stopped and watched his silver-grey eyes scan the area outside the barn. Seeming satisfied, he closed the door, sealing us in darkness once again. He guided me back to the bale and sat me down firmly.

"Ye still haven't accepted it yet? Ah'm not like ye."

"But you must be. It's crazy." I tried in vain to read his expression.

Saying nothing, he reached out for my hand with his, while his other tugged up the bottom of his thick sweater. "What will it take?" He pulled my hand up beneath the chunky knitted fabric and my fingertips skimmed across his tight stomach. After all the running I'd expected at least a sheen of sweat on Dom's skin but his was a dry heat. Soon, I felt what I assumed he wanted me to feel, a rough patch of skin on his left side, just below his ribcage. His hand stopped and held mine there as soon as he felt me react to the change of texture.

"How did you get this?"

His voice dropped to a barely audible whisper. "Ah told ye. Got it the day ma family were killed."

"Yesterday, in your room. The newspaper clippings. Someone saw an injured man, a naked man, staggering away from the scene." I felt a tremor run through his body and a splash on my forearm. "You're really him, aren't you?"

Dom remained silent but his huge frame wracked with silent sobs. I snaked my hands around his waist and up across his back, embracing him while he cried. His arms coiled around me in return and the big man sobbed into my neck.

Whatever Dom was feeling, he'd been channelling it into trying to identify his family's murderers, and allowing my father to control him through fear of losing what little he had left. I felt certain that his aggression was born from his suffering. What must it feel like to be alone? My own feelings of isolation withered as I considered this. I might have felt alone but at least I was human. What must it be like for him, I wondered?

Sometimes, when I was upset, Beth didn't say anything and let me cry. I stroked the back of Dom's head and waited patiently. He cried for a long time but his hold on me didn't relax once. Finally, the heaving of Dom's shoulders lessened and his hold on me loosened a little. I reached up and wiped the moisture away from his eyes.

"A'hm scared," Dom said, his voice cracking.

"I know. We both are."

He released me and loped to a bale opposite, sat down and put his head in his hands.

Without thinking I crossed to him and stroked his mane of hair, thickened with the salty night air, but smooth as always. "What was that, just then, in the water?"

"Don't ever go ontae the beach again. It knows ye're here now and it's coming for ye."

"What is?"

Dom leapt to his feet, grabbed me by the arm and dragged me to the barn door. He opened it a crack and peered outside.

"Maggs was right. We have tae get ye oot of here, off the island."

"Why? What was that thing?"

"Ah think it was the Nuck, like Millie told ye. Evil has risen, Leven, and it's coming for ye."

I would have scoffed at this had the fear in Dom's face made me feel colder still. "But why would it want me?"

"Ah think it's safe, come on."

In an instant, we were back in the house. When Dom satisfied himself that everything was secure, he finally loosened his grip on me. I shook my arm out, feeling the sensation slowly come back into my fingers.

"Follow me," he ordered, bounding up the tight staircases. "Ye need tae hear this from one of yer own."

I did as he told me. Halfway up the staircase I pulled my pendant out of my pocket to put it back around my neck. If it did offer protection then I needed all the help I could get. As I looped the cord around my neck, I looked down at the iron lump and stopped my ascent. One half of it had rusted where the varnish had been chipped away. Only Shaun would have done that. I remembered him saying that if it had rusted it would have been the same colour as his hair.

My reverie was broken by Dom pounding on the door to my father's room, his fist a mallet. "Mackay! This beuy of yers needs some answers." I had no idea why he bothered to hammer on the door because he shouldered it open without waiting for a response. It gave away more quickly than he'd expected and he stumbled into the room before swearing loudly.

I sprinted up the final steps and gasped at the horror that lay on the bed.

CHAPTER TWENTY-ONE
FATHER & SON

Mackay's body lay twisted almost out of recognition.

Dom crouched down and picked up the bedside lamp that, still lit, lay on the floor. As he set it back on the table, the light cast equally twisted shadows on the walls.

I stepped forwards gingerly and looked around. Mackay's catheter had slipped out and urine pooled on the floor, the acrid smell pervading the room. I covered my lower face with my hand.

Mackay looked even more insect than human and I noticed how much more frail he had become, even since our first meeting. He looked like a desiccated spider covered in tissue-thin skin.

"Is he. . .?" I couldn't finish the sentence.

Dom pressed his fingers against Mackay's neck then jumped backwards when the old man took a sudden breath.

"Leven." He tried to reach out to me. His arm twitched but wouldn't move. His bony fingers clawed at the sheets as he tried to pull himself upright. I felt the urge to help him up but I was reluctant to touch him. He looked fragile but there was still something malevolent about him. At first I thought it was because of the resentment I felt towards him but here, in this room, I felt a dark energy. "Dom, leave us."

Dom hesitated. He looked at me sideways, unsure of what to do until I nodded my assent to him. Although I felt deeply uncomfortable, I doubted Mackay was going to harm me. Dom backed out of the room, shut the door behind him and descended the first staircase. His footsteps ended there and I assumed he was listening from the landing.

Mackay's voice was a fractured whisper. "What do you know?"

"Dom told me that you took something from him. He can't leave without it. You're keeping him against his will."

"I need him."

"For what?"

"For what I'm not strong enough to do myself."

"But he says that you trapped him before you got sick."

His thin lips stretched across ragged teeth. "And what do you think of that?"

What the hell did he care what I thought? "It's not really for me to say."

"Come now, you must be thinking something."

"That you were. . .you know."

Mackay tried to smile but the effort only twitched the corners of his mouth. "What?"

Never had I imagined that I'd accuse my biological father of being bisexual. Why had I brought this up? The thought of it alone made me want to bleach my brain. I changed the subject. "He's angry."

"He's every right to be. He's an animal, caged and skittish. They sense when something bad approaches. Earn his trust."

"So, it's true? He's a Selkie?"

Mackay didn't have to answer. His gaze dropped. When he finally looked back at me his eyes were full of tears. Now Mackay changed the subject. "What do you know about you?"

"That I'm different."

Mackay said nothing. His shallow breaths sounded deafening in the overwhelming silence of the room.

"People don't want me here. They think I'm in danger."

"Maggs?"

"Yes. She doesn't think I'm safe."

"Stay away from the water."

I pointed out of his window towards the expanse of ocean. "Why did you bring me here if it wasn't safe?"

"You have to stop him.

"Who?"

"Your father."

"But. . .."

"Your real father."

Those three words alone made my breathing as shallow as his. I steadied myself against his bed.

Mackay continued as best he could. "The winter spirit. He rules the sea for half the year. He seduced my wife, your mother, before I could. She disgusted me then. You're their son."

"That's crazy." Then I remembered my last conversation with Maggs. "How can you be telling me this? Maggs cast a spell preventing it."

"Look at me," he rasped, his eyes indicating his withered body. "I've been trying to break her spell for years."

"Magic did this to you?"

"It's not meant to be used by humans." His left arm dropped off the edge of the bed and he winced in pain. I reached over him to place it back by his side and then I noticed something behind his bed; piles and piles of decaying books, shards of bone, trinkets, and a black metal bowl. All this time he'd been trying to get the truth to me, wherever I was. "The dog you killed," he wheezed. "You remember the dream?"

"That was you?"

"It was the only way I found to get to you. You are different. Show me."

"I don't know if I can. I've never tried."

"Take off the pendant. The iron dampens your demonic side. Remember your feelings from the dream. Try."

That made sense to me. The exposed iron had burned my skin. I pulled the pendant over my head and dropped it beside Mackay before picking up the black metal bowl from behind his bed and placing it on the floor at my feet.

Mackay watched me intently, only his eyes and chest moved.

My hand shook as I picked up the glass that sat next to his medication. I made a fist with my free hand and held it under the glass. As I concentrated on my feeling of fear from my nightmare, I slowly poured a trickle of water from the glass. Rather than splash against my fist the water curved around it and splashed into the bowl.

Mackay's eyes sparkled. "Your fear pushes it away. What does your anger do?"

I let the anger from my dream wash the fear away. As the water continued to trickle from the glass I turned my hand over, palm facing upwards. The water pooled above it until I made a fist and the water formed an irregular sphere floating above my hand.

A burst of sound shattered my concentration and the water washed over my hand onto the floor.

Mackay's wretched cough curled his body like a dying bug as he shook uncontrollably. I dropped onto the bed to help him but he thrashed violently.

"Dom, help me!"

"Lighthouse. S'all there," Mackay gurgled, then went still.

Dom bowled into the room and went straight to Mackay.

I stood and walked away to the corner of the room, unable to reconcile my resentment for Mackay with the realisation that he'd spent much of his life trying to get through to me, tell me the truth, warn me. To see him die like that, in so much pain, reminded me of Ruth and I realised once more that I'd tried to run away from my feelings but here they were, right here with me.

Dom reached out and straightened Mackay's limbs. I watched him, noticing how gently he placed each arm and leg. Despite the way he had been treated Dom still showed Mackay respect in his death.

As Dom positioned the final limb, Mackay's head lolled to one side. Fluid poured out of his mouth and onto his pillow.

I am five years old. The man who lives across the street is running towards me, shouting. He is running towards the dog lying at my feet.

"He's dead," the man begins to cry, struggling to lift the dog into his arms. The dog's head slips from the man's arms and water pours out of its mouth onto the yellow lawn.

"What's wrong?" Dom crossed to me.

"I've seen this before."

"Here?"

131

I shook my head, my eyes still riveted to Mackay's face. This was my nightmare made real.

Dom made a frustrated sound and started to search the room. I tore my gaze away from the body and watched him turn over each object one by one.

"Are you looking for your skin?" The words sounded strange even amongst all this strangeness. I started to feel numb, detached from everything that had happened in the last few days.

"No," Dom said, finishing a sweep of the room. "Ah'm trying tae work oot what happened."

"He drowned. Look at his face. See how sunken it is? He hasn't lost weight. The fluid from his body has been pushed into his lungs."

Dom stepped gingerly towards the body for a closer examination.

"Ye're right. But how-"

"Because I've done this."

Dom took his hands away from the body. "Ye did this?"

"Not to him."

"The dog." For the first time since we had met, Dom looked scared of me.

I grabbed my pendant and put it back on, tucking it between my vest and shirt so the rusted side didn't touch my skin. "We have to go to the lighthouse. He said it was all there, whatever that means."

Dom locked me in place with his gaze alone. "Ye'll see."

"Then let's go."

CHAPTER TWENTY-TWO
EVOLUTION

"Where are ye going? The lighthouse is that way."

"I need some answers from the only person who can tell me the truth."

"Ah can do that, moppy."

"Only about what you know. I need someone who knows everything."

"Who?"

"Maggs of course."

I set off at a pace but Dom soon caught up with me. We worked our way along the path towards the pub. The landscape seemed even more inhospitable. I glanced between the barren landscape to our left and the sea to our right. The rocks jutted more fiercely than yesterday, the waves chopped like blades, the dim light colder.

"She was only doing what she thought was right," Dom said. He sounded uncomfortable.

"I'm not going to hurt her but I sure as hell want that spell lifted. I need to know everything. Mackay spent years trying to get through to me. He killed himself trying to undo what she did. She needs to know what she-"

I heard a sound, a snort, behind us and spun around.

It was just a horse and its rider in the distance. I sighed with relief until it moved. The horse's legs looked like they'd been put together by a child. The joints moved too unnaturally for it to be a horse and the rider's legs skimmed the scoured grass. No, not its legs, its arms.

I stood motionless, my mouth agape. Where the horse's head should have been, there was a deformed lump with one red eye and a gaping mouth. The entire creature appeared to have been flayed. Two flame-red eyes in the second head fixed onto me and I gasped for air as a feeling of pure hatred washed over me.

The creature roared and galloped towards us. I couldn't move. This wasn't a story, a blue light floating over a deserted house. This thing defied explanation but here it was. I could see it. I could feel its hooves pummelling the ground.

"Run," Dom roared, as I felt his fingers hook under my arm.

My mind snapped back into focus and I ran. Dom was accelerating away from me fast, down the slope and onto the beach. He reached out behind him but his fingers closed on air. I couldn't keep up. Realising I wasn't right behind him he looked around, first at me and then past me.

He leaped into the air and spun to face me, his legs flexing as he landed firmly in the sand.

I heard the sound of snorting behind me. The horror of the approaching thing powered my legs as I sprinted towards Dom who was steadying his stance as if to fight it.

The creature shot past me and slammed into Dom, galloping towards the wall of rock at the back of the bay. It had him in its grasp, lifting him over its deformed head. Dom roared with pain as it threw him against the rock, the bare muscles of its hugely deformed arms twisting with exertion.

"Run!" His voice fractured as the creature struck him with a foreleg.

I ran, not away, but towards them. I'd run away for far too long. Now it was time to fight.

Dom wrestled against the creature, his eyes clamped shut with what I could only imagine was unbearable pain. When he opened them he saw me approaching and screamed for me to turn back but I knew I had to do something.

The thing's arms were held out straight, choking Dom against the wall. Its hooves dug deep into the sand as it leaned with all its bulk against him. Before I could get there Dom made a horrible choking sound then went limp. Distraught, I launched myself at the creature, connecting with its arms. The gigantic head snapped at me as I tried in vain to prise open its grip on Dom's limp form.

Black veins pulsed along the creature's arms. I lunged at them frantically, pulling on them whenever I was able to gain hold. They were tough but some burst, the foul stench of the thing's blood stabbed my lungs but it shrieked in pain and dropped Dom.

Then I ran, the beast in angry pursuit. I had to draw it away from Dom. Its attack looked powerful enough to have killed a man but I prayed that Dom was as tough as he looked and, after all, he wasn't a man at all. Maybe Selkies could live without air longer than a human or had some other way of breathing?

At the water's edge, I vaulted up onto an outcrop of jagged rocks before I risked turning to check where my pursuer was.

It was in midair, its front hooves and arms aimed squarely at my torso. I had no time to react and the connection exploded in my chest before I felt the rocks slam into my back. My pendant had come loose from my shirt. Still attached to my neck, it bounced on the rock next to my head. The creature roared in triumph and aimed one hoof at my skull. As it punched down towards me I dodged and the hoof connected with the pendant. It shattered and one shard pierced my cheek. I cried out in pain and kicked out at the creature, my feet connecting with the flesh between its forelegs. It staggered back, momentarily stunned. I flipped up onto my feet and took a step towards it, looking for some exposed artery to rip open but was distracted by a brilliant blue light in my lower peripheral vision.

The creature took advantage of my pause and struck my chest again. I heard my sternum crack before the pain crushed my vision and I soared backwards. For a brief moment I thought I could see everything. The beach, monster, Dom, house, pub, and millhouse. Everything looked bright, detailed, but so, so small. I knew I'd strike the water at any moment. My back began to prickle and then the world turned black.

I am five years old. The big, scary dog always barks at me. It is not only barking now. It is running towards me, its sharp teeth bared. I am scared. I know it wants to kill me, just like it killed that other dog.

My hands clench and I concentrate. The dog stops barking and slows down, its body moving towards me only because it is too big to stop. It falls to the floor, its head ploughs into the crispy grass and it flips over. It stays still now. Its fur looks dry in the burning sun.

I know that it is dead and that I have killed it. I took the water from its body and pumped it into its lungs.

The man who owns the dog is shouting at me and scoops the dog up in his arms. The dog's head slips from the man's arms and water pours out of its mouth onto the yellowed grass.

I hear someone run up to me, pick me up and carry me away. I can't take my eyes off the water trickling between the dead blades of grass. It is moving towards me like it's alive. I reach out. My hand looks different, older. Water rushes in from behind me, lapping against the body of the dog, which looks much bigger now. But this is not rainwater. This water smells of the sea. What am I doing in the sea?

The person carrying me away calls me by a name that I do not recognise.

I tried to roll over but something bulky stopped me. I opened my eyes to see the morning light illuminate Dom's face half-buried in the sand, his neck purple and black from strangulation. I raised my head and hand to check Dom's breathing and the movement brought him to life, his body crouched over me as he examined me with concern.

"I thought you were. . .." I said. "What happened?"

"Ye don't remember? Ah came roond in time tae see the Nuck-"

"The Nuck?"

"-knock ye intae the water. There was a sound, a boom, as ye hit the water. Ah thought ye lost. The sand was covered in something thick and sticky that smelt like blood. There was a terrible shaking of the groond and then there ye were, floating above the waves. Ye reached oot with yer hands and the Nuck keeled over ontae its side. It just dropped down dead. Then ye fell back intae the water."

"I killed it?"

"Aye. Ah crawled tae the water's edge and ye were there, babbling tae yerself aboot that dog. Once Ah had the strength Ah dragged ye back here."

"I killed it."

"Ye're Fin-folk. Ah ken these folk. Ye have the power of the storm. Something must have happened when ye hit the water. Ye've never been in the water before, have ye? Maybe that's why. Maybe it woke something in ye."

"Growing up I was always aware of water, where it was in the house, even in other people's bodies. I only managed to control water once, when I was in danger. A dog was attacking me. I drowned it. I was so scared at what I'd done I never used my powers again until the fight with Shaun's dad and last night with Mackay. He told me to use my fear and anger. I never needed to until I thought I saw you dying last night. I don't think it was the sea that caused this; I think it was the fear of losing you to that monster."

But Dom wasn't listening. His expression changed as if he'd remembered something. "And now A'hm going tae lose ye."

"What do you mean?"

His eyes flickered downwards to my chest and back to my eyes. He bit his lower lip. "Ah ye in much pain?"

I started to look down but he caught my face in his hand and warned me with his eyes. "Ye're hurt awful bad."

I pulled his hand away and examined my body. "Oh God." I could barely tell where the Nuck's blood, black and sticky, ended and mine began. My shirt was torn and hung away from my chest revealing an open wound. I felt faint when I caught a glimpse of bone. The cord of my pendant trailed out of the deep gash. I started to pull gingerly at the two ends of the cord but Dom's hand closed over mine.

"Don't. Ah tried while ye were unconscious. It won't budge."

He stroked my hair and I started to cry.

"Losh, moppy," Dom said, stroking my hair. "Don't upset yerself. It's going tae be all right."

But I had to get the pendant out of me. I pulled on the cord again. It resisted, glued into place by clotted blood, but then a wet pop and it moved freely. I pulled it out but the pendant didn't follow. Two useless strands of cord dangled from my fingers. It had snapped. I tossed the pieces aside and wondered what to do next. If I was clean I might be able to see the iron shard embedded in my flesh.

I rubbed away my tears with a filthy sleeve. "Can you take me to the water?"

Dom hesitated.

"Please?"

He lifted me carefully, carried me to the water's edge, but then paused. "Ah haven't been in the water since. . .."

Now I held his face in my hand. "You'll be fine, I promise."

He took a step and paused again. I'd never seen him look so uncertain, vulnerable. He caught my gaze and smiled humourlessly. "Who's the coward now, eh?" He gritted his jaw and took another step.

I soon felt wetness on my back and Dom cradled me in his left arm while he cupped his right hand into the water. He bathed my face and chest, cautious not to rub the skin. My wounds tingled.

"You bathed my hand in seawater, didn't you?"

He nodded while he worked. "It's a great healer for people like us."

"Like us?"

He looked back at the island and then to me. "Well, ye're not exactly human are ye?"

He bathed me while I lay in his arms in silence. Dom was right; whatever I was I wasn't human. Maybe that's why I'd always struggled with my temper, never fitted in, but I had connected with Ruth and Beth. I had loved them and I knew that they had loved me too. But London may as well have been a million miles away. The new life that I found myself entrenched in might very well be slipping away from me.

Dom finished cleaning my wound and he examined my chest closely.

"Can ye see it?"

He leaned in closer but the movement dipped me further into the sea. The water washed over my body and into my gouged chest. At once a blue light illuminated his face and his silver eyes sparkled against the grey light of the overcast morning. "Starnlight," he whispered, mesmerised.

The tingling in my skin grew and I felt a sudden rush of warmth spread through my body as if Dom had wandered into a sunlit patch. Then a feeling of deep calm surfaced in my thoughts. My lungs opened and I took a deep breath. Tears welled up in my eyes again as I breathed out, as if all the pain and sadness was being cleansed from my mind.

For the first time since Ruth's death I felt hope. The warmth in my chest intensified.

Dom waded back out of the water and set me down at the back of the beach, sitting up with my back against the rock face. He placed his hand on my chest and swore softly under his breath.

"Ah don't believe it."

I covered his hand with mine and moved it gently away. My wound had healed except for a low, smooth dome of blue stone that stopped the skin from reforming completely. I tapped it with my finger and felt my sternum thud beneath it. Was it fused to me?

"What happened?" Dom said, eyeing my chest.

"I remember my pendant shattering, then there was a blue light, it distracted me and then the Nuck knocked me into the water."

"Do ye think it was inside yer pendant all along?"

"Must have been."

"Where did ye get it?"

"My mum gave it to me. She said that it would protect me. It was from. . .." I realised then that the pendant, sent by Auntie Margaret, must have come from Maggs. She had another question to answer.

"Yer eyes shone like blue fire." Dom said the words thoughtfully as if trying to make sense of what he knew. When his eyes strayed from his reverie and focused back onto me he looked at me like he'd never seen me before.

His mouth was on mine even before I realised he'd leaned closer. It wasn't the hard, forceful kiss that I'd imagined Dom would give but one of a man tasting a foreign food for the first time, fascinated but hesitant, all too ready for it to taste wrong. My hands crept into his as he kissed me again, his expression thoughtful, but I could feel Dom's physical reaction; the pulse in the balls of his thumbs, his breathing getting faster. Dom kissed me a third time before I had the courage to kiss him back. Our only contact was hands and lips.

When we finally drew back, the sky had lowered, thick and heavy.

"We should find Maggs," I said.

Neither of us moved.

My gaze locked into his. "What are you thinking?"

He brushed his lower lip with his thumb and smiled. "Ah'm wondering what ye've done tae me and how tae stop it."

"You want it to stop?"

He looked away, his eyes back on the water. "All Ah've wanted for so long is tae find ma skin and leave. Tae swim as far as Ah could, tae be greeted by ma own kind. But now, if Ah'm left here and ye leave. . .." His hand squeezed mine and he looked down.

I squeezed his hand in return. "I'm not going anywhere."

He looked at our entwined fingers. "Since Ah pulled ye from the water Ah've felt strange. Thought it must be that it was the first time Ah'd been back in the water since, ye ken, but Ah found it hard not tae look at ye. Ah held ye when Ah got ye tae safety. Tell me, is it magic?"

"What do you mean?"

"Have ye done something tae me?"

"If Mackay had been good and kind would you have stayed?"

"Ah don't understand."

I was reluctant to try and explain the concept of love with Dom and it felt absurd to assume he had fallen for me. Clearly his feelings were alien to him and I wondered if he'd kissed anyone before.

I looked up at the horizon where dove-grey clouds darkened into a slate sea. I felt the tug from the water again but this time it felt sinister, like something evil beneath the waves had recognised me. "Come on."

We walked towards the pub in silence. Dom led me back onto the path towards the little building. I stole a few glances up at Dom's face but his expression was unreadable, lost deep in his unshared thoughts.

As we left the path for the pub's approach Maggs appeared in the porch, her worried expression striping her ruddy complexion with pale frown lines.

"What have ye done!" she demanded from Dom.

"He killed the Nuck."

Maggs looked at me aghast and steadied herself on a vertical beam. As short as she was, it was easy to tower over her but I still drew myself up as tall as I could. "I need answers. Lift the spell."

She didn't move.

"DO IT."

CHAPTER TWENTY-THREE
THE AULD HOOSE

The pub was empty save for Tammie and Millie who chuckled with each other by the fire. I pulled my jacket around me to cover my chest. When they saw us the lightness left their faces replaced with concern.

"I need to be alone for a moment," Maggs said, locking the door behind us. She smoothed her skirts down with her little red hands and then bustled out of the bar.

Neither Tammie nor Millie moved. They watched me intently, their gazes briefly flicking to Dom who stood next to me, one hand on my back.

Maggs reappeared some time later. "It's done."

"Who was my father?"

Tammie shifted in his seat, Millie looked at the floor, Maggs remained mute.

"You have to tell me now."

"No, I don't," Maggs said. "The spell prevented anyone from telling you the truth assuming they wanted to. If we don't want to, nothing will make us."

I closed my eyes and concentrated. My senses skipped from pump to pump along the bar until I found what I was looking for; the bar gun. There was enough fluid in it for me to grab hold of it and wrench it from its anchor. Water sprayed into the air before I caught it and held it in place.

Tammie swore.

When I opened my eyes a cloud of water hung above the bar. Most of the colour had drained from Maggs' face, leaving just the tip of her nose red.

"The sound of the winter gales-" Millie started.

"No," Maggs cried.

"He needs to know," Millie insisted. "They say the sound is not the wind, but his screams. His power is strongest in winter, causing the storms that batter our islands year after year."

Dom nodded as he listened.

"He rules the sea for half the year until the Sea Mither returns every spring to undo his damage."

"The what?"

"She calms the water in the summer," Tammie chimed in despite Maggs' ferocious glare. "Since these islands were formed their powers have risen and fallen every season until the year the Sea Mither did not return."

"Where did she go?"

"We don't know but that summer Mackay introduced us to his bride." Millie let the words hang in the air and it occurred to me that I didn't have to concentrate to keep the water there. My subconscious seemed to have it under control.

"You didn't know her?"

Tammie looked solemn. "We'd never seen her before and between us we know everyone, on every island."

Millie continued. "Mackay was vague about how he'd met her and she herself refused to be drawn on her past. Her pregnancy showed too soon for Mackay to be the father and ended too soon for it to be natural."

Maggs darted forward, anger boiling her face. "He was a beautiful baby."

Millie looked past Maggs and examined me closely. "Yes, he is."

Maggs whirled to face me. "She was so weak, Michael. So sad. She'd spent so long protecting us she wanted to walk among us. She never imagined that Teran would disguise himself as a man and-"

"Where is she now?"

"She returned and defeated Teran the following winter," Tammie said. "But we could tell she wasn't the same. Her power faded as her sadness grew." He jabbed his walking stick to the dark window. "And now we live with this." As if on cue, thunder rumbled in the distance.

"Why does Teran want me?"

Maggs dabbed her face with a bar towel. "His obsession with her extends to ye. Ye're his only child."

All eyes turned to Dom as he stepped forward. "Ah think it's more than that. Ah was building something for Mackay."

"Building what?" I asked. "Is that was the millstone was for?"

"Aye. When it was finished he said he'd give me ma skin back."

Millie leaned forwards. "What was it, Dom?"

Before he could reply, the colour drained out of Tammie's face. "The Odin Stone."

Millie whistled and shook her head in disbelief. "Maggs," she said. "Pour me a pint." She squinted over at the growing cloud of water that loomed above the bar and pulled a face. "Leven, do something about that, will you?"

An hour later, Dom sat perfectly still on a worn sofa that threatened to collapse under his weight. His hands cradled a glass still full of beer despite Tammie and Millie being on their third. They conferred with Maggs in a corner. From what little I overheard they debated both Teran's motives and what to do next.

I'd left them to it and gone upstairs to get cleaned up. Maggs had appeared briefly to offer me some clothing of her late husband's, muttering an apology and disappearing back downstairs before I had a chance to ask her about the pendant.

Now I perched on the edge of the sofa, cradling my own glass. I assumed that Dom had he been listening to the elders from here and nodded off.

I jumped when I heard a whisper.

"What," Dom's voice was hoarse. "What have Ah done?"

I put my glass down and knelt on the sofa next to him. "Did you know what it was?"

He shook his head. I took his glass and set it down next to mine before I reached back up and hugged him.

"Ye smell like meadows, moppy," he mumbled as he hid his face in my chest.

"Come on." I took his big hand in mine. "You need some rest. You're exhausted."

We made our excuses and Maggs showed us to our rooms. She'd closed down the bed and breakfast side of the business months before following her husband's death.

"Sleep well, beuys." And she was gone.

Dom frowned. "It feels different here."

"I know. It's strange."

"Ah don't like it."

"Do you want to stay back at the house?" We had moved Mackay's body out to the barn but I still hoped that Dom didn't want to go back there.

"Ah want tae be with ye."

"Are you sure about that?"

He threw his hands up. "Ah don't recognise maself. Ah don't know why but Ah want tae be with ye. Ah don't feel in control."

"Do you still think I'm doing something to keep you here?"

"Aye. No. Ah don't know. Ah know it's wrong."

"Wrong?"

"Thee and me. It's not right."

"Things have moved on, you know. Society is much more accepting of two men-"

Dom cut me short with a sudden laugh. "Is that what ye think this is aboot? Ah don't care aboot society. Ah'm thinking aboot me being what Ah am and ye being what ye are. How is this going tae work? Ma home is the sea."

"So you keep saying but you must have been curious about life on land otherwise why would you have befriended Mackay?"

"He took ma skin."

"Eventually, I know, but no one could make you make friends at the pub and become a member of the community, could they?"

"Ah needed tae get away."

"That's funny because I thought it was the sea you wanted to get away to."

"Ah like the people here."

"So stay. Do you have community out there? I don't think you do. Does anyone, anything, care about you out there? I don't think so. But I do. I care about you. But do you care about me?"

"Ah can't."

"Why not?"

He stepped back from me, his palms held up in surrender. "Ah haven't the words."

"Then show me."

CHAPTER TWENTY-FOUR
RELEASE

I stood at the bottom of the bed and towelled myself dry. Dom lay asleep, sprawled across the bed, making it look much smaller than it actually was.

I'd seen another side to the big man last night. So much of the past few days had been filled with Dom shouting, thumping, or crashing around the house in a temper that I was surprised to see how tender he could be. He handled me like a precious object, stroking my skin and kissing me all over. I'd only experienced Shaun's nervous admiration although I always doubted since then that he had ever really cared about me.

But Dom was different. Every touch of his hands and lips had telegraphed his wish for my pleasure. He kept eye contact with me constantly, checking my reaction to his touch, smiling every time I gasped with pleasure and pushed my hips off the bed. Then he would back off and try a new place to caress or kiss. It seemed like hours before Dom actually touched my cock. When he did I thought I might pass out; such was the sensation of his warm fingers on my shaft.

"It's so hard," said Dom, delight dancing in his eyes.

"If you keep touching me like that, I'm going to come."

Dom stopped, uncertain. "Is that bad?"

"It is if you don't get to feel what I'm feeling first."

I took my time exploring Dom's body. I had spent so long watching the way he moved, how graceful he was despite his size,

147

that I'd never stopped to think how he might feel. Dom was solid muscle, almost hard to the touch. My hands felt the thickness of his neck as I kissed him before resting them on his shoulders while my mouth moved across his chest.

But wherever my mouth travelled my hands followed. As my lips worked their way down the flattened bumps of Dom's abs his cock bounced upwards towards his stomach.

I breathed in the smell of Dom's shaft. It smelled of the ocean. I couldn't recall Dom ever bathing but he had spent time in the water. That unmistakeable saltiness, mixed with the strong smell of his cock, made my own shaft painfully stiff. I knew the big man was ready.

Moving up the bed, I extended my arms and raised my body up, a frozen push-up over Dom's body. Only our chests and cocks touched. Dom's hands clamped themselves around my arse and he ground his shaft against mine. I looked down to see drool from my cock drip onto the head of Dom's, joining his own pre-cum and pooling on his stomach.

I felt dizziness wash over me as Dom continued his persistent grind. My eyes became heavy and my breath caught in my throat.

It happened then; all my strength centred in my core and it was all I could do to keep my arms straight as my energy channelled itself into my cock.

The force of my ejaculation surprised us both, squirting scattershot within the narrow gap between us. Dom started to come, his own spurts thicker but just as powerful. His fingers dug harder into my buttocks as we jerked together on the bed. I regained my breath just long enough to cry out, finally falling onto my elbows for respite.

I buried my brow into his neck, my damp hair sticking to my own skin. My breathing slowed as I recovered but I could still feel our cocks pulsating and I felt eager for more.

But we fell asleep, exhausted both mentally and physically. I'd woken the following morning to find myself pinned to the bed by one of Dom's hairy forearms. I watched him sleep for a while, his expression neutral, before wriggling carefully out and taking another shower.

Now, as I stood at the bottom of the bed, marvelling at his magnificent physique, he suddenly sat up and pulled me onto him.

"What are you doing?" I said, as Dom's hands explored mine.

"Ah'm checking yer hands."

"For?"

"Webbing."

I swatted his hands away, pretending to be mad. "You are a bad man."

"Ye're the bad man. Ah'm not even a man."

"Man? You usually refer to me as 'boy'." I couldn't imitate his accent.

He grinned and I wanted to kiss his smile at once. "Or 'moppy'."

"I'd rather you called me that than 'boy'." I wriggled into his lap and kissed him again. He tasted of animal health and I let my tongue roam over his blunt, square teeth before seeking out his own.

As Dom returned my kisses his hands explored me, the warm pads of his fingers making me shiver when they traced the sensitive curves of my lower back.

The only thing that distracted me from his mouth was the delicious sensation of his hooded cock prodding mine.

I rocked back onto my haunches, spat into my hand and daubed the fluid across Dom's cock. He gasped at the sudden touch and his hips bucked involuntarily.

I spat again, reaching behind me to slide my fingers inside myself.

Taking his cock in my wet fist, I tried to ease myself onto it. Dom inhaled sharply and grabbed my waist when he realised what I was doing.

"Can we do this?"

I smiled down at him and he relaxed with a smile unlike any I'd seen before. It was a half-smile, his eyelids heavy. His bottom lip seemed fuller, too.

I eased myself down again but Dom, his hands back on my arse, lifted me off him to kiss and lick my chest. He savoured my taste.

I had thought so often of the mechanics of this moment I'd never considered what it might feel like.

Despite his tenderness last night, I thought he might use this to prove his dominance over me but now any doubts I'd had were gone.

Not that I didn't have something to prove. "I want you inside me."

He reached around and rubbed a finger across my hole. I writhed in the grip of his other hand, eager for more contact with his fingers. He pushed the tip of his finger against me and smiled when I opened for him. I made a small sound when I realised that my cock had begun to drool again; a thin line of fluid ran down the shaft of my cock and dripped off my balls onto the base of Dom's.

"Please," I begged, pushing against his finger.

With increased force, he worked his finger deeper inside me. His probing digit felt hot against my flesh. He introduced another finger and worked me with both. So that was it, he wanted to fuck me but suspected the head of his cock would prove too blunt a tool to pierce me that easily.

Apparently satisfied that I was ready, he picked me up. His head swung between the bed and the wall before he decided on the bed. I'd never imagined that he would ever want me like this, especially like this, and I surrendered to the idea of Dom consuming my flesh with all his strength and power.

Laying me carefully on the bed, he pushed my thighs back and lapped at the place his fingers had been moments earlier. I shuddered when he made contact and again when he slid his thick tongue inside me.

I muttered something to God. The reaction spurred Dom on and he pushed deeper inside me, twisting his tongue this way and that, enjoying the stream of incoherent moaning I couldn't control.

Weaving my fingers into his hair, I pulled him away from his taunting game and up to my face. With my legs wrapped tightly around him I looked into his eyes.

"Do it." The aggression in my demand surprised us both.

Dom spat into his palm and fisted his cock, but it was already slick with his pre-cum. I hoped I was wet enough to take him as he rocked his hips towards my eager flesh.

It took all my concentration to open up to him so he didn't hurt me. Dom slid into me until I felt the snap of my ring back around the head of his cock. He stopped then, feeding me an inch more before pulling back and checking that I was okay with a cautious look.

He looked down and I felt his cock throb, no doubt aroused by the sight of his thick rod in my hole. He slid in an inch further but pulled back again, this time so my ring opened up again and over his head. Just before he was clear, he pushed back in, very slowly this time, and one inch more. He continued to fuck me with the first few inches of his cock, his eyes locked to mine at all times.

Then he withdrew and sat back, gazing down at me. His skin glistened, light dappled across his solid build.

I met his look with one of complete surrender. No words were needed for my request and his eyes answered it.

Dom slid back into me again and I fought the urge to scream. He towered over me, his big hands clamped around my shins. I could feel every thick vein on his magnificent cock as he slid into me. As much as I tried to relax I couldn't stop my balls from tightening and my cock from straining upwards. I had never been fucked and was glad Dom had taken control and lubed me up so well. His big, flat tongue had worked wonders on my muscles, allowing me to relax enough to take him.

Light caught Dom's shoulders and part of his face as his head lolled back. Clearly, he was enjoying the complete penetration too, sliding the last few inches into me. The fucking started then; long, slow strokes, painfully slow at times. Dom let go of my legs and curled his body over me.

I wrapped my legs and arms around him, kissing his hair, his brow, his lips. His tongue was soon working against my own and the sensation of both his mouth and cock threatened to take me over the edge. The sound of our kissing was joined only by the soft slap of skin on skin.

Dom changed position, still pushing into me but with his arms straight and hands firmly planted either side of my head. I watched his abs contract with each thrust. I rocked myself back, using his powerful shoulders for support, and wrapped my legs further up his body. The angle allowed even deeper penetration and I knew I'd come soon. A steady stream of pre-cum dripped onto my chest.

I needed this. In every move we made together my muscles burned with the effort of restraint. I could have come as soon as he entered me but I wanted this to last for as long as possible. For all I knew I could wake one morning to find Dom gone, his skin retrieved. If this was the only time we'd have together, to truly be together, then I had to make it count for something, to make it as good for him as it felt for me.

But my body could not be denied. When I wrapped myself tighter around him I knew I could last a few minutes more at the most. Seeming to sense my turmoil, Dom slowed his thrusts but that did nothing to slow the approach of my orgasm.

I knew Dom's next stab into me would be the cue for my release. He pressed deeper into me as his cock swelled to be even thicker, soon followed by the first hot flood of liquid. I started to come, splattering my chest and neck as Dom's continued pressure curled me tighter and tighter. The moment seemed to have no end, each contraction of my arse, balls, and cock triggered the same in Dom. It felt like the cum that Dom pumped into me somehow flooded through my own balls and out through my cock.

Dom's mouth connected with mine unexpectedly, hungry for my open mouth, as if to devour me in this moment of pure abandon. The big man's mouth moved to my chest, licking up beads of juice and transferring them to me. I ate hungrily.

Feeling Dom's thrusts subside I relaxed into the kisses, allowing my hands to run down the slick pads of muscle covering his back.

Dom started to withdraw, albeit still hard.

I reached around and pulled him back inside.

"No, stay."

He laughed gently, withdrew anyway, and rolled us onto our sides. I pushed back into his embrace and stroked his arms.

"Have ye thought aboot what tae do?"

"Yes, I thought about it all night long."

"And?"

"I'm going to the lighthouse."

"There are forces greater than either of us at work here. Ah don't know what will happen-"

"I'm still going."

"Ah felt energy there and was convinced it was ma skin."

"I thought you said it was at the house?"

"Ah ken that, so it might be something else."

"The Odin Stone?"

"Maybe. Or it might be another Selkie's skin. Ah've never been withoot mine before. Ah don't know what it feels like and never asked."

"You're not the first?"

"Selkie women have been tricked by men into becoming human wives then fled back tae the sea as soon as their skin is found."

"Have you ever met one?"

"No. They tend tae keep away from men after that; avoid ships, stick tae deep water. They're never the same afterwards. Torn between the two worlds Ah guess."

"How come?"

"They served as wives, mothers. Living as a human is not all bad."

"How do you feel?"

"Ah don't know. Mackay tricked me and Ah never felt the same about him again but then he got sick. Ah thought that if Ah stayed here then he might take pity on me and let me go. Or if he died Ah could find ma skin."

"Assuming it's even here."

"It might be at the lighthouse."

"Will you leave when you find it?"

Dom let go of me, rolled off the bed and stood up. "Ah don't want tae talk aboot it."

The look on his face convinced me that the matter was closed. This wasn't Maggs' spell; he didn't want to tell me. My heart sank. So that was it, he was going to go as soon as he found it. I didn't like to see Dom agitated but was also aware that I didn't know him well enough just yet to push the matter further.

I held out my hand, took his and squeezed it to convey whatever I could.

Dom smiled, kissed me and left the room. I assumed he'd gone to look for his clothes that Maggs had insisted on washing.

I admired the view of his retreating body and felt my cock harden again. I hoped there'd be plenty of time for that in the future.

CHAPTER TWENTY-FIVE
THE LIGHTHOUSE

The noon sun hung low in the summer sky but hid behind thick cloud as we stepped out into the fresh air. I was glad to be outside and thought of the Sea Mither making her way back to the ocean to take her place. I wondered where she went in the winter. To warmer seas elsewhere? To roam the land in search of me, her lost son? I wished I had a mother out there, making her way back to me. My thoughts turned to Ruth and how she would make a fine spirit for good, always finding the best in everything and everyone around her. I still missed her but the pain wasn't as sharp as before.

Since my baptism in the water I felt different. At first I thought the turning point had been my night with Dom but now I felt certain it was something more. The stone's warmth ran through me, lending fluidity to every sense of my being. My thoughts still washed over each other but without confusion. They blended into each other and created a clearer picture of everything around me.

Dom put his arm around me as we walked away from the pub towards the north of the island.

"Are ye sure ye want tae do this? It could be dangerous."

"I have to. I don't know why. It feels right."

I allowed my hand to flatten out at the botom of Dom's back, the ball of my thumb resting in the deep vertical trough at the base.

"Ah suppose ye need answers."

"I'm not looking for answers anymore. I'm looking to do what's right. Millie thinks the Odin Stone was destroyed for a reason and I agree."

"Ye think Mackay wanted its power?"

"No. I think Teran does." My eyes flicked to the blackening sea. "He might be coming for me but I think he's coming for the stone, too."

Dom stopped walking and turned to me. "Ah don't want ye tae go. Who knows what might happen if ye face him? He might have recovered the Nuck, restored its power and be waiting for ye."

"Then I'll kill it again and properly this time. I'll be fine, I promise."

Dom didn't look convinced but he turned back in the direction we had set out in.

"Ah'm coming in with ye then. Ah'll make sure ye're all right."

"That's not what we agreed."

"Ah don't care."

We rounded an outcrop and Dom pointed upwards. "It's up. . .."

I looked up as his voice trailed off. I'd expected a white tower with red stripes but the structure that loomed above us looked like a vast, melted candle. A blanket of dirty, opaque ice covered the entire structure, feathered with ridges. I couldn't make out any of the original building.

"But Ah was only here the other night," Dom said, mystified.

"Do you think he's here already?"

Dom wasn't listening. "How will we get in?"

"Can't you do what you did with the millstone?"

"Ah've never done that with a person, moppy. What if it hurts ye?"

"It doesn't hurt you, does it?"

"No, but-"

I grabbed his face and kissed him. For the first time his skin felt cold in the bone-chilling wind. "Then I'll be fine."

He hugged me tight and buried his face in my hair. I nestled into the thick wool covering his chest and closed my eyes. I couldn't hear him say the words but I felt his jaw move against my scalp.

As he spoke my body became light and I felt energy radiate from his body into mine. I saw a bright channel of light in my mind and felt my body jump. The light shunted sideways followed by a powerful white flash.

I took a breath and a strange chemical smell greeted me. I opened my eyes slowly. We stood in a cool, dark space. I was grateful to still be encircled by Dom's embrace. Waves of heat emanated from him again and I felt calm considering I had no idea what might be waiting for us.

Dom drew me closer. "Now, Ah'm going tae show ye the Odin Stone. It might frighten ye but ye need tae see it." Dom's voice was soft and reassuring. "No harm will come tae ye here, Ah promise."

I nodded, guessing that Dom could see me clearly although everything remained in inky blackness to me.

Dom moved away, his departure causing swathes of cold air to replace him. I shivered and drew my jacket tighter about me. The air in here felt like the air in the cave; damp, wet, bitterly cold. I heard the strike of a flint and a faint hiss then Dom's massive silhouette loomed before me. Behind him, shadows danced across an old brick wall.

The brickwork curved up and over us reminding me of an arch under a viaduct. To my left and right I saw what appeared to be benches covered in boxes, in turn covered by dust sheets. In one corner stood a taller box, roughly the size of a phone booth. Abandoned building materials were scattered about and I remembered Tammie telling me that the builders had walked out when they discovered Mackay's plans to turn the lighthouse into apartments. I doubted that had ever been his intention. He just needed the place gutted.

The lamp in Dom's hand lit his face from beneath, making even his encouraging smile look demonic as he beckoned me over to him.

"The tower's through here." His hand hovered above the handle of a low door. "Ah'll check it's safe then call ye in."

I swallowed hard and nodded.

He opened the door and walked through. As he turned to my right I ducked my head through the doorway.

My mouth fell open. Huge chunks of stone floated in the air, slowly rotating around a vertical axis. The room smelled like fresh rain and my hair crackled with static the way it did in the winter. The occasional discharge of energy arced between the stones as they drifted past me. I spotted the millstone among them, turning slowly as if spinning underwater in slow motion.

Dom had completed his circuit of the tower and approached me from the left. He laughed at my hair and reached out to touch it. As he did so, a sliver of energy erupted from my chest and connected with the lamp he held. The stones halted and started to draw closer together before popping back out, a wave of energy throwing us both backwards through the doorway.

Dom landed awkwardly on me and I cried out in pain. He rolled away before springing back to my side.

"Are ye hurt?"

I grabbed my upper arm which he'd landed on and winced. "I'm fine." I managed a smile and patted his leg. "Don't worry." He started to speak but I cut him off. "How come I can see you?"

He'd dropped the lamp when we'd been thrown from the room. It lay twenty feet from us, extinguished, but the room was bathed in a pale green light.

Dom looked for the source of the light as I sat up and shook my arm. By the time I got to my feet Dom was standing in front of the booth-sized box in the corner. He reached up, grabbed the sheet covering it and pulled it away to reveal a glass tank filled with cloudy green liquid. I hadn't known what to expect. A fridge? A fortune telling machine? I stood in front of the tank, vaguely reminded of a derelict fish tank taken over by algae. A green glow emanated from within.

Phosphorescence?

I looked at Dom, confused. "Have you seen this before?"

"No." He handed me the sheet and shimmied down the side of the tank, reached out to hook his fingers behind the upper half of it and tilted the tank forwards. Judging by the grinding of his teeth it was heavy and awkward. Still, I reasoned, he'd lifted a millstone only a few nights before.

Seeing nothing, I held up the lamp and took a step towards the glass. Still nothing. Finally, I leaned in so close that my brow met the glass as it tilted towards me. Something in the water reacted to me. I saw a movement and the glow pulsed.

I stepped back. The core of the tank remained dark. Squinting my eyes to dampen the glow I made out the rough shape of a figure suspended in the verdigris sludge.

Dom grunted and pulled harder. The figure drifted forwards slowly, its arms coming up slightly as if to embrace me.

A body thunked gently against the glass, the face eye-to-eye with me.

I fell against the boxes behind me. Now my own core turned dark. Dread surfaced and I pulled the sheet to my chest as if to smother it.

I knew the face opposite me. I saw it every day.

It was my own.

CHAPTER TWENTY-SIX
FAMILY

The sound of my vomiting reverberated off the wall just as the vomit itself splashed across my boots. As soon as my guts emptied I gasped for air, catching sight of Dom appearing beside me. He breathed heavily and I guessed he'd set the tank back upright instead of just letting it go.

"What did ye see?"

I couldn't form the words. My hand unconsciously went to my chest and my fingers touched skin. Confused, I looked down and saw that the energy discharge from my chest had burnt away the layers of fabric. My skin was intact and the blue stone pulsed in time with the phosphorescent liquid in the tank.

Without looking up I pointed to the tank. "It's me."

Dom made a sound in the back of his throat but said nothing. I could hear his boots creak as he shifted his weight from foot to foot. Was he unsure whether to stay by my side or investigate?

I grabbed hold of his closest thigh and hauled myself to my feet before making my way to the tank. Dom joined me and sucked in a breath over his teeth when he saw the face.

I looked at my twin. I couldn't think of him as anything else. "I think he's my brother. Maggs found my mother on the beach. She was weak. Maybe she'd already had one child and Teran took him?"

I tried to imagine what his life had been like. He'd had at least one of his parents. I wondered what Teran was like, even a monster could be a good father, and then I remembered Gerald. That monster was certainly not a good father. Shaun seemed a lifetime away now. My anger towards him had drifted away with all my other negative emotions.

My brother and I already shared one history; we had both been secrets. My own mother had hidden me away from Teran. I had been kept a secret by Shaun's parents so that Shaun wouldn't spoil their name and reputation. And I had hidden myself away from the world after Mum died. The Sea Mither had kept my brother a secret from Maggs. In turn, Teran had kept him from the world. Assuming Mackay had known about him he'd also kept him concealed here.

Mackay was right. I was discovering the truth here.

I heard movement behind me and looked over my shoulder to see Dom opening, one by one, the vast number of boxes in the room. He worked feverishly and I knew he was looking for his skin.

I wondered how it must have felt to know your real family and then lose them. At least he had known their love. But I had known Ruth's love and I was thankful for that, no matter how short-lived it had seemed. Alex was another matter and I knew I had some work to do to salvage our relationship assuming I made it out of here alive.

When I noticed Dom's sudden stillness, I turned in his direction, distracted from the tank. He held a bundle in his hands and I saw him trembling from the other side of the room.

"Is that. . .?"

Dom nodded mutely.

I ran to him and stared down at the bundle. The skin was covered in a loosely-woven fabric, tossed into a pile of filthy rags like an old garment.

"Had you searched here before?"

Dom looked at me, his eyes wide and liquid. He seemed completely distraught.

I caught his jacket and tugged it hard. "We have to get it out of here and somewhere safe. That pulse could have been a beacon. Teran could arrive at any moment. Come on."

But Dom just stood there.

"Come on!" I pleaded, panic rising in my chest.

"Moppy," Dom started. "Do ye love-"

But he didn't get to finish. A bright light filled the room as the door exploded inwards and a monster rose from the wreckage.

CHAPTER TWENTY-SEVEN
TERAN

The creature stood taller than Dom, covered in black armour that reflected the light like a beetle's shell.

Flattened by the blast, I shook my head to recover my senses and looked for the source of the light. It streamed through the doorway. The shattered Odin Stone was shining brightly and I realised that the humming in my ears wasn't the result of the explosion but a wall of sound emanating from its core.

When the monster started to move I saw that its armour comprised of a series of interlocked chitinous plates and its back and head was shielded by a menacing carapace.

It was humanoid.

"Fin-man." It was all Dom said as he darted forwards and pulled me back to where he was huddled under one of the benches.

Dom had called me that yesterday after I regained consciousness on the beach. If he recognised that in me then it meant that one of these things had fathered me.

I felt both revulsion and fascination. The Fin-man looked dangerous but it radiated a magnetic power that held my attention as I watched it move around the room. It stopped when it reached the tank and made a sound like disgust before moving on. The parallel benches gave it little option but to weave up and down each aisle. It would be upon us soon and I knew it would notice us.

I tensed, ready to run, but Dom's hold on me tightened. "Ah'm not letting ye go," he hissed into my neck.

Damn him, I thought. I had offensive power. I'd killed the Nuck. Even though I hadn't used it consciously I did have it in me. If I was threatened it might manifest, take over and destroy the Fin-man itself.

I closed my eyes and concentrated, trying to conjure my fear and anger but I felt the stone in my chest begin to work against me. Its soothing energies gathered in my thorax and I felt them expand outwards. No, I had to push them back and access the chaos that I'd inherited from Teran.

Gritting my teeth I focused on my anger at Shaun, at Mum's death, Mackay's, and Maggs' interference. I recalled my fear seeing the Nuck pummel Dom against the cliff and then how enraged I had become.

The blue energy faltered within me and I drove my anger into it. As it collapsed in on itself I tore myself free from Dom's grasp and stood up.

The Fin-man froze when it saw me. Its vaguely human face, just eyes and a mouth, looked startled.

Now the anger took me for itself. I raised my hands towards the Fin-man and prepared to unleash death upon it but I stopped when I saw my hands. They were covered in the same plating as the Fin-man but shot through with veins of blue crystal. I hadn't even felt my transformation but it didn't scare me.

"Who are you?"

I shouldn't have been surprised that the monster spoke; it had a mouth and looked as much like a man as anything else.

"I'm Leven." My voice sounded different, a deeper register. Even the mechanics of my throat felt different. I couldn't feel my tongue but somehow I'd managed to say my name.

The Fin-man sniffed the air and stared at me in shock. "I sense her in you."

I knew exactly who he meant so I knew who he must be; Teran, my real father. The Sea Mither was his enemy as well as his obsession. She'd defeated him in an endless cycle of seasons so she had the power to subdue him. If I had her power as well as his I might be able to kill him.

Unexpectedly, his shoulders dropped and he loped away from me towards the tank. When he reached it he put one hand on the glass, his fingers splayed outwards as if to calm the figure within. "I thought there was only one."

His height allowed him to rest his armoured head on top of the tank. He stood motionless then, without warning, drew his arm back and punched his way through the front of the tank. "I needed you both!"

He grabbed the body as it lurched towards him and threw it against the opposite wall. So that had been my brother. My anger rose again just as it had when Dom had been thrown against the cliff but this time there was no opportunity to charge Teran for he had launched himself at me.

"Run!"

It was all I had time to yell at Dom before Teran's roar drowned out the Odin Stone itself.

"I needed you both!"

I had no idea what his plan had been but its failure enraged him. His impact dwarfed that of the Nuck's and we tumbled across the room as he battered his fists against me. I covered my head instinctively and waited for the world to stop spinning.

His assault continued after we struck the far wall but his frustration scattered his blows randomly across my armoured body. It hurt but he wasn't injuring me as far as I could tell. This new body was going to take some getting used to.

As quickly as he had attacked, he disengaged and I felt the disturbance in the air as he leaped away from me. I couldn't see Dom anywhere but Teran was heading back towards the tank, one arm extended.

The spilt green water that once imprisoned my brother rose up at his unspoken command and lurched towards me. I had no time to evade it but no fear of it either. It was just water. But when it struck me I imagined I had been stabbed. The water had crystallised and the shards had penetrated the gaps between my armour plating.

I cried out with pain and fell to my knees, gasping for breath through my distorted mouth.

Teran's gurgling laugh heralded a second attack as he drew the crystal shards from my body and dug them back into me. I thought that my brain would shut down from sensory overload.

Surely this much pain would make a man faint? But I wasn't a man now. I was the son of the Sea Mither and a Fin-man and I had powers of my own.

Now I had to surrender my anger and fear to the blue energy that marbled my new body.

It was harder than I'd expected. Teran's proximity seemed to fuel the power I'd inherited from him. As hard as I'd fought to suppress the blue energy, now I had to fight to draw it back out.

Teran sneered at me and raised his hands again, mouthing silent words.

Immediately the room began to shake. Objects fell from the benches, boxes toppled and the room filled with dust. I heard Dom coughing but I couldn't see him through the thick air.

I accessed my chaotic power and lashed out in Teran's direction. I could feel the water in my invisible grasp and wrestled to keep it in shape as I flung it back at him.

The water cleared the air between us but Teran reflected it back at me with a wave of his hand. The crystallised slab hit me square in the face and pain shot through my skull. Blood blurred my vision, stinging my eyes.

I gathered my strength and tried to drag myself onto my knees. What I wouldn't have given for some training but I could feel the raw power surging back through my body. I might have been battered and bloody but it fuelled me, as did my hatred.

This thing had single-handedly caused all the pain and hurt in my life to bring me to this moment. If he'd been human, and I had no power, I'd gladly have cut the fucker's balls off with a rusty razor blade. Slice, slice, plop. I'd watch the bastard writhe in pain as I worked.

Fuck him. Fuck every useless family that had fostered me. Fuck the cancer for killing Mum. Fuck Shaun for being weak. Fuck Teran for seducing my mother and killing my brother. Fuck everything.

"Time to die, you cunt."

I drew a deep breath and concentrated, feeling the moisture in the room around me; the damp in the floorboards, beneath the footings, in the crumbling plaster on the walls, and the brick behind it.

I sensed the water in Dom's body, the blood pumping through it. I had to shield him from what I was about to do.

A mist formed around me, the collected droplets drawing towards me from everything I'd sensed apart from Dom.

Dom appeared beside me, looking around us as noises of cracking and splintering sounded all around us.

"Leven?" he said, his voice quavering.

"Now might be a good time to get out."

The blue energy crackled around me, illuminating the mist cloud from within. Teran backed away towards the doorway but stopped suddenly, gripped by my invisible hand. I directed the cloud towards him and forced it into his mouth and eyes.

"What are ye doing? He can breathe water."

"He's not keeping it."

Teran writhed and twisted in pain. His legs buckled beneath him but he didn't fall. I held him in place.

"Ye're killing him."

Teran grasped at his throat and tried to speak. I was certain that he had killed Mackay in front of us but Mackay's lungs were filled with water from his own body. I was pumping Teran full of additional fluid that his body shouldn't be able to contain. He stopped struggling but I continued to focus all is energy on him.

"Stop it. He's gone."

But my focus was unbroken. "Not yet."

I lifted my hands, palms up flat and then pulled back. Teran's armour cracked and turned wet as blood sprayed from his wounds.

"Enough, Michael. Enough."

My power died within me and I realised that the voice that had been instructing me was not Dom's.

A gentle voice made a placatory sound and a hand touched my forehead. Only Ruth calmed me like this but a cascade of blonde hair and a pair of sparkling blue eyes gazed up at me.

"I am your mother."

CHAPTER TWENTY-EIGHT
SUMMER

I watched her as she turned away and walked across the room to the doorway. At some deep level I recognised her but the feelings I imagined at our first meeting didn't surface. Not yet, anyway.

She was beautiful but she was cool, detached. I reminded myself that she was not human.

I had no strong feelings towards her and questioned if this was the part of her I'd inherited. It must be inhuman to be so calm that you felt almost nothing.

Alex had tried to cut off his feelings but they still bled through. Mum had worn her heart on her sleeve for the world to see. And then there was Dom, a torrent of emotion. He was as wild as the Orkney winds themselves.

That was how I'd felt after accessing my powers and defeating Teran; a surge of emotion amplified my power and in turn it elevated my emotional state. They fed off each other, my emotions and my power.

We followed the Sea Mither into the tower and she began to speak, her voice soft as if she was unfamiliar with forming words.

"Teran's Fin-folk covet these islands more so than any other creatures in these waters."

I cringed at the thought of anything else apart from the Fin-folk, Selkies and the Nuck being in these waters. Dom wasn't the last of the Selkies, I knew that. How many other creatures lurked out there?

"Teran now knows of your presence here. You could replace Lorcan in his plans."

"Lorcan?"

"Your brother."

So he had a name. "Teran said he needed us both."

She paused, her face passive.

Dom's voice broke the silence. "Ye must protect him, Mither!"

The Sea Mither glanced at him briefly before returning her full attention to me. "May I speak with you alone?"

Before I could respond, Dom left my side. "Ah'll keep an eye on Teran."

She looked after him as he left and then took my hand. It was an awkward gesture, as if she had seen someone do it once and thought it the right thing to do. "My sojourn into the human realm was an attempt to gather my strength to defeat Teran for all time. I did not realise that it would be my downfall, that he would exploit this human's weakness against me and have me sire his children."

I drew my hand away from her light hold. "This human?"

"This is not my body. I am only spirit."

"So that thing I was killing-"

"Is a Fin-man possessed by Teran's spirit."

I had achieved nothing. I'd destroyed something that Teran only controlled. There could be thousands of Fin-men for him to send after me.

The Sea Mither continued. "I knew human love. I loved you both as I carried you and for the short time I held you in my arms. Letting you go was the only option I had to protect the islands."

"I'm trying to understand, but-"

She held up a hand. "But that is a memory now. I recognise only one side of you, the spirit side. I am not human. Since my return to the eternal struggle my human feelings have gone. I do not say this to hurt you."

Her words didn't hurt me. Although she appeared human I sensed her alien attitude towards me. She was not the mother I had fantasised about.

"I had a human mother who loved me very much."

"Can you forgive me?"

"For giving me up?"

"Yes," she paused again. "And for what I am about to ask of you. Teran's only weakness may be you yourself. When Teran took Lorcan for his own he raised him to take his place but as he grew his powers proved to be weak. Teran tortured him in a bid to twist his mind against me and sent him to kill me. It was a foolish plan and I killed Lorcan before he could attack. I sent his body back to Teran as a warning."

"How could you kill your own son?"

"He was no longer the child I gave birth to. Would you have let him destroy you?"

I knew she was right but her attitude still seemed brutal. There was no remorse in either her expression or voice.

"You have great power," she continued. "Was this always so?"

"No but it appears when I am scared or angry. When I was young-"

"Then it comes when you need it most." She seemed satisfied by this. "I wished for a sign or a prophecy that foretold your arrival but there was none. Now I see you my hope returns."

"What do you think Teran wants?"

"He wishes to possess me and he wishes for greater power. How he plans to achieve this I do not know."

"Why do you think he needs the Odin Stone?"

"The Stone o' Odin was used for many years to bind promises. The island folk swore oaths upon it and believed it granted them protection from disease but its true purpose is to bring balance."

"But if Teran becomes more powerful than you won't the stone restore balance by increasing your power to match his?"

Dom strode back into the room, dragging the semi-conscious Fin-man behind him. "Sea Mither! Teran meant to transfer your powers to Leven and his brother!"

He dropped the Fin-man and gathered me up in his arms as the Sea Mither examined the broken body he had discarded behind him.

"Teran has left this body to perish," she announced.

The Fin-man's blood seeped from his wounds and soaked the wooden floorboards that strained under his weight. I knelt beside him and cradled his head. "I'm sorry."

His deep green eyes rolled upwards in their sockets and his mouth dropped open. In my half-remembered dream I had enjoyed killing the dog but now I felt nothing but anguish. I had taken a life that on its own may not have wished me harm. This poor creature had been used by an evil spirit and I had shattered its body with a power inherited from the same foul thing. I felt disgusted with myself.

Dom crouched next to me and put his arm around me. I tried to shake him off but he pulled me closer still. "Ye had no choice, moppy."

"I'm sick of death."

He didn't speak but put his face into my hair and wrapped his other arm around me. It occurred to me then that my head was no longer covered by my carapace. When had I changed back to my human form? I clung to Dom and wished that he would transport us out of here and back to London but, before I could ask if that was even possible, the entire tower shook.

Dom and I sprang to our feet to see the Odin Stone shift sideways, the floating chunks threatening to break free and crush us all, before the central core pulled the pieces back into place.

The Sea Mither's face turned heavenwards. "Teran approaches."

CHAPTER TWENTY-NINE
SACRIFICE

The tower shook again and I heard a thunderous crash outside. The ice was breaking up and falling down around the building. Another crash sounded in the room attached to the tower and a cloud of dust billowed through the doorway as shards of ice scattered across the floor.

The Sea Mither darted up the spiral staircase that jutted out of the tower's internal wall. It didn't seem like a good idea to me. If the tower was going to collapse, was being at the top a wise choice? Then again, being at the bottom when it collapsed seemed even more stupid.

Before I could decide for myself I felt Dom's hands on my back, pushing me after her.

The staircase proved to be as unsafe as it looked. No sooner were we high enough that a fall might prove fatal than a step gave way under Dom's weight.

He dropped quickly but my new reflexes were faster. I caught the wrist of his up-stretched arm and held him fast. The step beneath me groaned under the weight but held just long enough for me to haul him up and move forward.

The Sea Mither had no such problem and leapt from step to step with ease. I watched her ascent towards the top of the tower where the lamp was housed. But before she could reach the top of the staircase and climb into the lantern room the entire structure was sheared off just above her head.

She covered her head and cried out as something reflective narrowly missed her. I caught a glimpse of a huge glass lens fall past me and shatter against the tip of the Odin Stone.

I looked down as the glass fragments fell away and broke into smaller pieces as they struck the floor. From my vantage point the dead Fin-man looked like he had been covered in snow and ice.

My chest hummed with energy and I pulled at the tear its previous discharge had ripped through my clothes.

The tip of the Odin Stone droned with a new frequency and, looking down, I was shocked to see that the core had turned the same shade of blue as the stone fused to my sternum.

I realised what I had to do. If there was any chance that Teran could use me then I had to stop him. If I could restore the Sea Mither's power then she could subdue Teran. If the Odin Stone brought back balance then I'd have to sacrifice myself to complete Dom's work.

Dom followed my gaze and looked at me in horror as he realised what I was considering. "Leven, no!" He caught hold of me and tried to pull me back from the edge of the step on which I perched. I tried to free myself from Dom's grip but the effort was a token gesture. I was scared and Dom knew it; I could see that much in his expression as his grey eyes tracked over my face. "Ye can't leave me."

I held his face and answered the question he hadn't been able to finish when he found his skin. "Yes, I love you." I pushed away from him and jumped into the air. I was a diver now, an Olympian, and I wanted gold. I turned in the air, muscles flexed; as I'd watched my heroes do for so many years. I knew I was going to die but the fear left me as quick as it had come.

The Odin Stone pierced my chest and pure blue light exploded within me.

CHAPTER THIRTY
BURIAL AT SEA

Death was a beach, lit dimly by a sun that wouldn't set. My last memories rushed back to me and my chest began to heave with emotion. I cried out into the silence. The stone in my chest was gone, an angry scar the only evidence of its strange attachment to me. It had been the last piece of the Odin Stone which now stood whole, inert, among the remains of the lighthouse high above me on the cliff. Chunks of the building also lay around me on the sand.

So this wasn't death. I had survived somehow, naked but alive.

I dragged myself to my feet but immediately fell again, skinning my knees on the rubble. They bled freely but I ignored them. I had to find Dom and make sure he was safe. I pulled myself up again and concentrated on my legs, keeping them planted firmly between the remnants of lighthouse and gouged sand.

The quiet unnerved me. I had become used to the constant squall of the wind and its never-ending push and pull. This evening was calm, what Dom said the Simmer Dim should be.

I scanned the ruined shoreline for signs of life but saw nothing moving. Seeing a ragged bundle, I clambered over the rocks towards it, but it was only a dead sheep. Seaweed still hung from its mouth. The poor thing had been crushed mid-meal. Its blood had stained the sand around it. As I followed the fading mark to the water's edge I saw a lump of tattered leather and cried out in panic.

There was no doubt it was Dom's boot. I clutched it to me and fell to my knees again. I was angry at myself for assuming the worst but I had lost so much already why would today grant me a reprieve?

My search became feverish. My eyes stung from my tears and again from the sand I worked into them as I carelessly wiped those tears away. I had to find him. I pulled at piles of wreckage until my fingers bled but I didn't care. I stooped only to tug a broken fingernail from its bed but the pain was nothing compared to my rising terror.

I saw the ragged bundle of Dom's skin first, still clenched in his fist. At least he died reunited with the one thing he'd spent his human life searching for. I was certain he was dead. No light danced in his eyes which stared vacantly at the sky. No air filled his lungs. No pulse drummed in his chest.

I sat beside him while I decided what to do. What would Dom want? He had spent all his time looking out to sea so it seemed fitting to take him out into the waves but he'd also wanted to stay with me.

I made my decision and dragged his body towards the sea.

My only choice was to take him out into the water and stay with him until the sea took us both. I didn't know what might be waiting beneath the surface for me. I didn't care. All I wanted was to be with Dom in his natural element.

I had no idea how the skin fitted to him. The shapeless thing bore no indication to suggest if it was to be draped or wrapped around the body.

Dom was heavy but I was able to undress him and roll him in the supple skin until he was cocooned inside it, just his beautiful face still visible.

Once in the water, I worried that his body might sink but the skin swelled and remained buoyant enough to help me swim us out into deeper water. Surprised by the power of my strokes, and unused to the strength I gained from the sea, I looked back to see that the islands were simply distant breaks in the horizon.

I stopped swimming and cradled Dom in my arms. As my tears fell onto his face I sang the lullaby that Tammie had sung to his dog in the pub.

"Ba, ba peerie t'ing, sleep a bonnie nappie; thoo'll sleep an' I will sing, makin' lassack happy".

The sun was at its lowest point now but the deep orange orb offered no warmth as we floated beneath it. I finally felt myself tire, my legs kicking more and more slowly.

But I held fast onto Dom, resting my head on his chest and singing softly.

"Ba, ba lammie noo, cuddle doon tae mammie; trowies canna tak' thoo, hushie ba lammie, hushie ba lammie, hushie ba."

Then everything closed around me and I was wrapped in something else.

Darkness.

CHAPTER THIRTY-ONE
THE GIFT

"Ye have to eat something."

"Go away and leave me alone."

Maggs sighed and took a step closer to me. I moved away, the bedrock uneven beneath my feet.

"Ye're weak, beuy."

It only took a look over my shoulder for her to see I was in no mood for persuasion. She placed the dish down between us and backed away.

The morning sun beat down on me and I cursed it under my breath. I longed for the grey skies and churning waves but I was denied. Since the Odin Stone's completion balance had been restored and the weather fell back into its normal pattern of ebb and flow.

I was certain that it had killed both Teran and the Sea Mither and sensed neither of their influence within me. Balance had been restored not by levelling their power but by removing them completely.

But I remained as always, counting my losses.

Millie had found me washed up on the east coast of the island during one of her daily searches but there had been no sign of Dom. I remained unconscious for several days until Tammie thought to give me a seawater bath which revived me.

That was three months ago.

I scowled again at the late September sun. It made it more difficult to pick out the waves from the bobbing seal heads.

I'd become a thing of curiosity for the local grey seals. They watched me intently, albeit from a safe distance. I could understand their distrust of men having read every clipping tacked onto Dom's bedroom walls. I slept in his room now, comforted by his smell which permeated the rugs and skins he had occasionally nestled himself into.

Beth had visited a month ago but even she failed to conjure a smile that reached my eyes. She didn't mention Shaun and neither did I. She brought me gifts and as I had opened each one I realised that she might be more than human herself. Knowing nothing about what had happened she had made figures of the Sea Mither, the Odin Stone and the frozen lighthouse. Her eyes grew wider than the ocean when I told her what had happened and she cried with me for my loss. She brought with her a letter from Alex full of emotion I never knew he possessed. He wanted me to come back home as soon as I felt able.

But I couldn't be persuaded and Beth returned to London alone.

As Dom had stood on the beach night after night so I stood on the rocks day after day. But just as he had been denied his wish so I was denied mine; he was lost to me.

Maggs cleared her throat. I had forgotten she was there.

"Leven," she said, finally using the name I preferred. "If he was alive he would have returned to ye by now."

"How can you possibly know that?" Deep down I knew she was right; I'd looked into his eyes and seen no flicker of life behind them.

"There are countless stories of Selkie-folk that return to thank those that helped them in times of need or freed them from imprisonment at the hands of another. He's gone."

"How dare you!" I couldn't bear to hear her say what I knew to be true.

"Please come inside and eat a meal."

"I'm not hungry."

"Then sit by the fire."

I neither moved nor spoke. Eventually she threw her hands up in surrender and retreated out of sight. This daily ritual was proving to become as eternal as my parents' had been.

I kicked the dish she had left behind. Cold porridge spattered the rock and was taken just as quickly by a wave.

I watched the dish bob towards me and then race back before deciding to snatch it from the ocean's grasp.

But my hand connected with something else snagged on an outcrop just under the waterline. The dish forgotten, I pulled the new object out of the water and staggered backwards.

It was a Selkie's skin. I recognised its supple texture immediately and drew it to my face. As the water streamed from it I breathed in Dom's unmistakeable scent and then roared at the water before me, my cry as guttural as the one I'd heard on my first night here.

"Give me back his body, you fucker!"

"Ye swear tae much, moppy."

Now I knew I'd lost my mind as well as Dom but at least if I could hear his voice I wouldn't feel so alone. I tilted my face to the sun and let my tears flow freely. When my gasps subsided I decided to go back to the house. There was no point waiting for him anymore.

But a man stood in my way, his huge head and shoulders blocked any sight of the house behind him.

I felt faint. "It can't be."

"Wouldn't ye like tae see yer loved ones again?"

I dropped the skin. "It can't."

"Even if they were just a light in the sky?"

I knew those words. "They don't come back."

Dom covered the space between us in a single stride. His fingers interlocked with mine and held them against the softness of his sand-blasted skin. I smelled the saltwater on his hair and saw the crystals forming on his collarbone. His breath was sweet and warm, just as I remembered it.

"Say it again," Dom whispered, almost inaudible over the sound of the waves.

"Are you staying?"

He squeezed my hands. "How is this going tae work?"

"The same way it does right now, with you here and me here."

"Ye're not going back tae London?"

"Why would I when you're here?"

"Say it again. Please."

"I love you."

His forehead fell onto mine, his eyes closed. "The night ye arrived Ah stayed oot all night, thinking of ways tae get away. Mackay told me nothing aboot ye so Ah thought ye might be some part of a plan tae keep me here forever."

"And now?"

"Now Ah never want tae leave ye again."

"Then you won't need this." I scooped up his skin and started to fold it up as if to keep it.

He looked at me in horror.

I threw it down between us and laughed as I tore off my own clothes and threw them on top. "And I won't need these."

I launched myself into the water closely followed by Dom who playfully tried to push me under. I twisted and swam away but he caught up with me and we eventually surfaced in each other's arms.

"Why did ye do that?" he said, grinning.

"To show you that I'm as comfortable out here as you are on land."

"But Ah bet Ah can oot-swim ye, moppy." He flicked water in my face and dove out of sight surfacing seconds later by the bedrock on which I had waited for him for so long.

As he hauled himself out of the water, I admired his back, the muscles shifting as they pulled him free.

I followed but I had the power to launch myself from the water and land gracefully next to him.

"Now ye're showing off," he chuckled and plunged his hand into the pile of clothes.

I looked down at what he'd handed to me. He'd given me his skin by accident. "This is yours Dom."

"Aye."

"But it's your skin," I said, confused.

He looked down at it in my hands and he smiled, his expression as soft as his voice. "Aye."

"But... why?"

"Because of the one thing Ah haven't said tae ye yet." He hooked his fingers around the back of my neck and drew my mouth to his.

The kiss was the longest we'd shared. I was lost in it, soothed by the lips I'd longed for and the feel of his warm body against mine.

When he finally pulled back the silver flecks in his slate-grey eyes reflected my devotion for him.

"Ah love ye, Leven."

THE STORY CONTINUES IN

MEMORY
OF WATER

Turn the page for an exciting preview…

AFTERMATH

I cowered in the corner, my hands over my face, curled into as tight a ball as I could. What the fuck? I swallowed hard but it wasn't enough to stifle a loud sob as I gasped for air. What the fuck just happened?

Bugbee and Powell had burst in, I remembered that much. There was lots of shouting and swearing. Powell had suddenly rushed me and pinned me to the wall. Bugbee made a move towards Leven and then…

I tried to control my breathing and risked a peek out from between my hands. The flat was trashed. Someone's remains smeared the walls and floor like a twisted makeover. I could make out clumps the colour of Bugbee and Powell's hair dotting the wet meat that lay in chunks on the floor. That left just me and Leven, who stood at the front door, his forehead resting on the peeling paintwork, his eyes closed. Was he even aware of me?

Acid rose in my throat just at the thought of what Leven had done in this very room. I'd pleaded with the men not to hurt him but they'd ignored me and started throwing their weight around. Leven sprang to life when he saw Bugbee advance toward him.

Now the men were dead and I was fucked.

I needed an exit. Images of the rooms flashed through my mind like a slideshow. There was a fire escape outside the bedroom window. With Leven blocking the front door it was my only chance. I pushed myself to standing and headed towards the hallway as carefully as I could, picking through the men's remains and not taking my eyes off Leven for an instant.

The hallway remained dark as I crossed the threshold and flicked the light switch. The power was out. Fuck. I looked around but could see nothing except the bedroom and bathroom doorways. If I tripped over anything I'd alert Leven to my presence and run the risk of being attacked. All that stood between me and my only possible chance of survival was twenty feet of open space.

Cautiously, I took a step forward, and then another and another. I was just about to break into a run when I felt hands on my shoulders. Leven spun me around and the look on his face buckled my legs. I fell, sprawled on the floor.

Leven towered over me, blood covering his face and teeth.

I suddenly felt awe at the sight of him. Raw power emanated from his core and his blue eyes glowed – fucking glowed - in the darkness.

Leven widened his stance and, behind him, I could see what was left of Bugbee's head, a trail of grey matter splattered behind the broken lump.

I felt like I was drowning.

"What happened to you?" I was so scared my voice cracked as I asked the question.

He raised his arms above his head and I saw the glimmer of metal in his grasp. "What happened to me?" His hands rushed downwards. "You."